Dance With Me

Jahnna Beecham

BANTAM BOOKS
TORONTO • NEW YORK • LONDON • SYDNEY • AUCKLAND

RL 6, IL age 12 and up

DANCE WITH ME
A Bantam Book / September 1987

ISBN 0-553-26701-9

Published simultaneously in the United States and Canada

---

*Bantam Books are published by Bantam Books, Inc. Its trademark,
consisting of the words "Bantam Books" and the portrayal of
a rooster, is Registered in U.S. Patent and Trademark Office
and in other countries. Marca Registrada. Bantam Books, Inc.,
666 Fifth Avenue, New York, New York 10103.*

PRINTED IN THE UNITED STATES OF AMERICA

O   0 9 8 7 6 5 4 3 2 1

DANCE WITH ME

Behind the dune, a dark-haired boy was bending over and scratching Brandy behind one ear. Brandy's tail thumped contentedly against the sand.

"Brandy!" Charley scolded, wagging her finger at the dog. "You bad boy!"

The boy in the jogging suit looked up and smiled. His eyes were a startling shade of blue, and Charley nearly gasped out loud when she saw them.

"I was jogging on the beach," he explained, "when I saw you dancing in the surf."

Charley felt herself blush, and she nervously smoothed the wet pleats on her shorts.

He had a tiny cleft in his chin and shining brown curls that the sun had streaked with red highlights. But it was his blue eyes—which were the color of the Gulf—that made Charley stand openmouthed, staring at him.

"Oh, I—I didn't expect to see anyone out here this early," she stammered. "Usually I'm the only one."

"I try to jog earlier myself, but I'm behind schedule today," the boy explained. "Oh, by the way, my name is Brett. Brett Murphy."

Bantam Sweet Dreams Romances
Ask your bookseller for the books you have missed

#1	P.S. I LOVE YOU	#107	IF YOU LOVE ME
#2	THE POPULARITY PLAN	#108	ONE OF THE BOYS
#5	LITTLE SISTER	#109	NO MORE BOYS
#18	TEN-BOY SUMMER	#110	PLAYING GAMES
#20	THE POPULARITY SUMMER	#111	STOLEN KISSES
#63	KISS ME, CREEP	#112	LISTEN TO YOUR HEART
#71	TOO MANY BOYS	#113	PRIVATE EYES
#77	TEN-SPEED SUMMER	#114	JUST THE WAY YOU ARE
#81	SECRET ADMIRER	#115	PROMISE ME LOVE
#82	HEY, GOOD LOOKING!	#116	HEARTBREAK HILL
#85	THE BOY SHE LEFT BEHIND	#117	THE OTHER ME
#88	WRONG KIND OF BOY	#118	HEART TO HEART
#89	101 WAYS TO MEET MR. RIGHT	#119	STAR-CROSSED LOVE
#90	TWO'S A CROWD	#120	MR. WONDERFUL
#91	THE LOVE HUNT	#121	ONLY MAKE-BELIEVE
#92	KISS AND TELL	#122	STARS IN HER EYES
#93	THE GREAT BOY CHASE	#123	LOVE IN THE WINGS
#96	FIRST, LAST, AND ALWAYS	#124	MORE THAN FRIENDS
#98	LOVE IS IN THE AIR	#125	PARADE OF HEARTS
#99	ONE BOY TOO MANY	#126	HERE'S MY HEART
#100	FOLLOW THAT BOY	#127	MY BEST ENEMY
#104	PLAYING FOR KEEPS	#128	ONE BOY AT A TIME
#105	THE PERFECT BOY	#129	A VOTE FOR LOVE
#106	MISSION: LOVE	#130	DANCE WITH ME

Sweet Dreams Specials

A CHANGE OF HEART
MY SECRET LOVE
SEARCHING FOR LOVE
TAKING THE LEAD
NEVER SAY GOODBYE

To my good friends, Linda and Kevin Cooney

Chapter One

"All ashore that's going ashore," a strong male voice called.

Charley Maclaine lifted her head and looked up into the grinning face of her father, who was peering down at her through the open hatch.

"My charter passengers will be here any minute. Besides, you'd better get a move on if you're going to go jogging and get to school on time." Even though she couldn't see him, Charley heard Brandy, their golden retriever, bark in agreement.

"OK, OK." Charley laughed good-naturedly, brushing a wisp of her dark brown hair out of her eyes. "I'll be right up." She slid the faded ice chest up against the bulkhead and lashed it into place.

"Captain Maclaine?" someone called out.

"Over here!" Charley's father called back over his shoulder. Then he leaned back down into the hold and whispered confidentially, "Looks like the gang's all here. Let's give these tourists a good show, OK?"

"Aye, aye, sir!" Charley grinned, tossing off a smart salute. She scrambled up the stairs and stepped out onto the deck.

The sun was just starting to lift over the horizon, and a cool April breeze off Choctaw-hatchee Bay sent a pleasant shiver down Charley's back. Her brown eyes glistened as she gazed out over the pink-tinged waters of the Gulf of Mexico.

"Welcome aboard *Peg o' My Heart*, gentlemen!" Charley's father announced cheerfully. The bleary-eyed fishermen, holding steaming cups of coffee, were gingerly climbing over the side of the boat.

"Captain Maclaine at your service," he continued. "The best charter fishing boat, as well as the best skipper, in Dalton Beach and quite possibly the west coast of Florida!" The four tourists nodded sleepily. Charley's father, whom everyone called Captain Mac, pointed toward the cabin and said, "You can stow your gear in there, gentlemen. We'll be under way in just a few minutes." The passengers stumbled off obediently, and Captain Mac turned back to Charley. "Did you remember to fill up the shrimp bucket at the bait shop?" he asked in a whisper.

"Of course, Dad!" Charley replied, rolling her eyes in mock disgust.

"That's my girl!" he said, wrapping his arm around her shoulders. "Best crew a captain ever had. Right, Brandy?"

The dog wagged his tail and let out a resounding *woof*. They both laughed.

"OK, now, over the side with both of you!" he cried, clapping his hands together. "Prepare to cast off!"

At the command the golden retriever leaped onto the pier and started running back and forth, barking excitedly. Charley jumped onto the dock and stood patiently by the mooring. Captain Maclaine clambered up to the wheelhouse above the cabin and flicked on the boat's diesel engine. It roared to life, rumbling throatily through the still morning. Charley's father then tossed the baseball cap he'd been wearing onto the seat beside him and put on an old-fashioned captain's hat.

"Cast off the bowline!" he bellowed. For the benefit of his passengers, Captain Maclaine liked to issue nautical commands, even though Charley knew very well what to do and when.

Charley stifled her giggles and expertly loosened the line, tossing it back onto the deck of the boat. She gave the bow a sharp shove with her foot, then ran toward the stern, Brandy barking at her heels. After she had tossed the aftline aboard, she called out, "Catch a marlin for me, Dad!"

Captain Mac did a double take and stared down at her incredulously.

"A marlin? A mere marlin?" he sputtered, striking a heroic pose with one hand pointing out to sea. "No small fry for this good ship. We won't be back until the White Whale is ours!" He spun the wheel with a flourish and eased the boat toward the open water.

Grinning from ear to ear, Charley waved until the vessel turned into the channel leading to the Gulf. From across the water, she faintly heard her father yell, "Tell your mom I'll be home for dinner at around seven o'clock tonight. And no fish!"

Charley kicked off her sneakers and ran barefoot down the beach. Early morning was her favorite time of day because the beach was empty. The occasional gung-ho surfer in a wet suit might be trying to catch a wave, but usually it was just Charley and Brandy.

Charley kept running, feeling the sand squish between her toes. Her shadow stretched out in front of her, mimicking her every move. Ahead of her, Brandy was trying to bite the rippling waves as they lapped at the shore.

A crisp breeze blew the clean, salty smell of the ocean into her face, and it tickled her nose as she breathed it all in deeply.

The rhythmic sound of the waves always made Charley want to dance, and she began practicing her grand jetés at the edge of the surf. She pushed herself to the limit, reveling in the power coiled in her long, muscular thighs as she sprang into the air.

"Run, run, *leap*! Run, run, *leap*!" Charley shouted, imitating her ballet teacher's commanding voice. Miss Carabelli ran each class with the discipline of a drill instructor, but her students adored her. She wanted only the best from them, and Charley loved rising to the challenge of pleasing her teacher. With each leap Charley tried to spring higher, tossing her head back with a wide grin. Brandy stopped and watched her curiously, his head cocked to one side.

Finally Charley paused to catch her breath, the cool edge of the surf curling around her ankles. She bent over, stretching her arms down the length of her slim, tanned legs. Grasping her ankles, she felt the pleasant ache of the stretch go through her hamstrings. As she was stretching, a small wave suddenly caught her by surprise, and she jerked upright with a squeal. Her shorts were soaked, and she automatically took a few steps back up the beach.

"Now for our pirouettes!" Charley instructed Brandy seriously. She tossed her ponytail back across her bare freckled shoulders and held her chin high, trying to look like a true prima ballerina.

"Ready, set, turn!" Charley commanded. She spun around on one leg in the sand, her arms wrapped in a circle around her. She figured that if she could complete a double pirouette in the sand, maybe she would be able to spin around four times in the dance studio.

Charley bit her lip and focused on a point on the horizon, ready to try her turn again.

Suddenly Brandy barked sharply and raced toward a nearby sand dune. As he disappeared out of sight, Charley shouted after him, "Brandy! Brandy, come back here!"

But her voice didn't carry against the roar of the surf, and with resignation she trotted after her dog to see what all the commotion was about.

Behind the dune, a dark-haired boy was bending over and scratching Brandy behind one ear. Brandy's tail thumped contentedly against the sand.

"Brandy!" Charley scolded, wagging her finger at the dog. "You bad boy!"

The young man in the jogging suit looked up and smiled. His eyes were a startling shade of blue, and Charley nearly gasped out loud when she saw them.

"I was jogging on the beach," he explained, "when I saw you dancing in the surf."

Charley felt herself blush, and she nervously smoothed the wet pleats on her shorts.

"I didn't want to intrude, so I ducked behind this dune," the boy added, grinning sheepishly. "But it looks like Brandy, here, found me out."

He had a tiny cleft in his chin and shining brown curls that the sun had streaked with red highlights. But it was his blue eyes—which were the color of the Gulf—that made Charley stand openmouthed, staring at him. He smiled at her, and even Brandy turned to pant expectantly in her direction. Charley suddenly realized she should say something.

"Oh, I—I didn't expect to see anyone out here this early," she stammered. "Usually, I'm the only one." She walked toward Brandy and began patting him on the head.

"I try to jog earlier myself, but I'm behind schedule today," the boy explained. "Oh, by the way, my name is Brett. Brett Murphy."

"Hi," Charley managed to answer. "I'm Charley Maclaine." She couldn't get over how handsome he was, and she hoped she wasn't staring too much.

"Charley?" he asked, looking perplexed. "That's different."

"Yes," she explained quickly. "It's short for Charlotte. But everyone has called me Charley for as long as I can remember—except for my mother when she gets mad at me. Then she calls me Charlotte Anne Maclaine—" Charley realized she was babbling and added jokingly, "Some people call me motor-mouth."

As soon as the words were out of her mouth, Charley felt like kicking herself for saying something so dumb. She bent over quickly and began scratching Brandy behind the ears.

Luckily, Brett didn't seem to think her remark was that goofy. Instead he laughed warmly, and Charley looked up into his eyes again.

"You know," he said, "you're really a good dancer!"

Charley blushed at the compliment. "I take ballet classes five times a week and try to jog as often as I can. It's supposed to strengthen your ankles, for dancing *en pointe*. Oh, en pointe is French for 'on your toes,' " she explained. Then she continued in a breathless rush, "This morning I was trying to perfect my pirouette by doing it in the sand. A pirouette is a turn like this." Charley started to demonstrate the turn but lost her balance in the middle of it and wobbled to an awkward finish.

"Well, it's not like that, exactly. It's . . ." Her voice trailed off as she realized Brett was grinning at her.

His eyes were full of amusement as he said, "It looked pretty perfect to me."

"So," Charley asked a moment later, digging her toes in the sand, "are you here on vacation?"

"No, I live here," Brett responded, brushing a stray lock of hair off his forehead. "I go to Choctaw High School."

"You're kidding!" Charley blurted out. "So do I!" She tilted her head and looked at him quizzically. "But I haven't seen you in the halls. I'm sure I would have remembered you if I had." Charley clapped her mouth shut as she realized she had put her foot in it once again.

"My family moved here a week ago," Brett replied easily, "but I've been meeting with my coach a lot in the last few days. I haven't really settled into classes yet."

"Oh, my gosh, school!" Charley yelped, looking down at her watch in alarm. "I'm going to be late," she cried. "Come on, Brandy!"

She backed away, stepping clumsily over Brandy, who was jumping around excitedly behind her. Charley recovered her balance, trying to look as casual and self-possessed as possible.

"I'll look for you at school!" she called out.

"Sure!" Brett answered, waving his hand. "See you around!"

Charley waved back and walked calmly around the dune until he was out of sight. Then she flew down the beach toward her house, her heart racing as fast as her pounding feet.

Charley charged through the kitchen door, letting it slam behind her. As usual, she forgot to brush the sand off her feet. "Charley, you did it again!" her mother called out.

"Sorry, Mom!" she called back, racing into her bedroom. She tore into her closet, pulling out three dresses and tossing them on the bed. A few minutes later Charley was scrambling around on her knees, trying to find her good sandals when her older sister, Amanda, sailed into the room.

"You are such a slob, Charley," Amanda said, sniffing haughtily as she stepped gingerly over an outfit Charley had dropped on the floor the night before.

Charley peeked out of the closet to look at her sister. Amanda always looked as if she'd just stepped out of a fashion magazine. Her golden hair framed her face perfectly, and she always put on just the right amount of mascara to make her green eyes stand out brilliantly.

"Sorry, Amanda," Charley apologized, backing out of the closet. "I'll clean it up later."

"You always say that," Amanda complained,

looping her purse over her shoulder and picking up her textbooks. "And I always get stuck doing it myself."

"Well, if you'd wait until I got back from dance class," Charley said defensively, "I could clean it up."

"Sure. Fine. And just how am I supposed to do my homework in this mess?" Amanda pouted.

Charley shook her head. She finally found her brown sandals and tossed them toward the bed. Then, dashing over to her messy desk, she shuffled through the stack of papers piled there. Charley found the essay she had written the night before and placed it hastily on the bed.

"Help me, Amanda!" Charley pleaded, turning around to face her sister. "Which dress should I wear?"

Amanda wrinkled her nose and airily pointed at the pink cotton T-shirt dress. Then she turned and floated out of the room.

I don't know how she does it, Charley thought, pulling her dress over her head and slipping her feet into her sandals. *I get up at six in the morning, and I'm always late. She gets up fifteen minutes before we have to leave and looks like a model.*

Charley hastily tucked a black leotard and a pair of pink tights in her canvas bag and paused briefly in front of the mirror to look at herself. Her hair was still in a ponytail, but she decided she'd fix it at school.

Just before she left, Charley glanced quickly around her bedroom. Amanda's bed was perfectly made, with little white-lace pillows arranged carefully along the headboard. Her desk was bare except for a reading lamp and a vase full of irises. Charley hadn't even made her bed, and it looked as if her closet had exploded on top of it. She couldn't remember what her desk looked like under all the papers that covered it. Old toe shoes and copies of *Dancemagazine* were scattered about the floor.

I really ought to straighten this mess up a bit, she thought guiltily. But just then an image of Brett and his dazzling blue eyes came into her mind. She wasn't going to waste time cleaning that day. Grabbing her dance bag, Charley headed for the kitchen.

"I've got dance class tonight," Charley said, not really having to remind her mother. She picked up a piece of buttered toast from the kitchen table as she ran out the door.

"OK, honey. You be sure to eat a good

lunch!" Charley's mother called to her daughter on the driveway. She stood in the doorway, holding Brandy by the collar. "I worry about you, Charlotte. You're too thin. Amanda, try to make sure she eats something nutritious."

"Yes, Mother!" they both chorused in singsong voices. It was part of their morning ritual. Mrs. Maclaine always hovered at the back door, shouting last-minute instructions and gesturing wildly. They watched her bring her hands in front of her and bump them together, reminding them to fasten their seat belts. Charley and Amanda waved gaily and hopped into Charley's beat-up yellow Volkswagen.

The little car, with its dented fender and torn upholstery, was Charley's pride and joy. Her parents had given it to her a few months before her sixteenth birthday. They had offered it to Amanda the year before, but she had refused it.

"I'd rather have a new car for graduation," she had reasoned, "than have a ratty one now."

Charley started the engine, waited a minute, then slipped it into reverse and backed out onto the street. She shifted into first, and soon the familiar buildings lining Santa Rosa Boulevard were zipping by the open window.

As they rode along, Charley debated whether or not to tell Amanda about Brett, but she finally decided against it. Amanda collected boys the way other girls collected stuffed animals, and Charley didn't want Brett to become part of her collection!

"Charley, hide me!" Amanda suddenly squealed. She ducked down below the windows, as Charley brought the car to a stop at a red light.

"What? From whom?" Charley stammered, looking around in confusion.

"On the corner!" Amanda hissed, raising one arm and pointing toward the curb. "He's over there!"

Charley looked over and saw Mike Cunningham leaning against a mailbox talking to some friends.

"I thought you were dating him," Charley whispered, trying not to move her lips.

"We broke up," Amanda whispered. "I'm seeing someone else."

"Who?" Charley burst out eagerly, slouching down to hear her better.

Before Amanda could answer, Mike spotted the car and loped over to the passenger window.

"Hi, Charley," he said, poking his head inside. "How's Amanda?"

"I'm just fine, Mike," Amanda replied, sitting up and almost bumping heads with him. She smoothed her hair and giggled nervously. "I dropped a contact lens."

When the car behind them let out a long, grumpy blast of its horn, Charley jerked her head up to see that the light had turned green. In a panic, she floored the accelerator.

"Bye, Mike!" they both called back as the little yellow car sped off down the street.

Charley turned to her sister. "Amanda, you don't wear contact lenses."

"Mike doesn't know that!" Amanda purred, smiling shyly.

As they pulled up in front of Choctaw High, four boys were already waiting for Amanda to arrive. Before she had even gotten out of the car, Skip Parker, the school's star fullback, opened the door and scooped her books up under his arm.

"Why, thank you, Skip!" Amanda said, burbling and flashing him one of her killer smiles. "You're so sweet to carry my books."

Charley shook her head in wonder, then pulled forward and turned into the parking lot. As she edged into an empty space, she spotted the tall and rangy figure of her best friend, Jiggs Reed, sitting on the hood of her pickup truck.

Jiggs and Charley had been friends since first grade, when they had discovered that they both had unusual nicknames. Jiggs's real name was Janice, but she never let anyone call her that. Janice didn't suit her personality, anyway. If Charley's passion was ballet, Jiggs's was horses. They always attended each other's concerts or horse shows and usually found some time every day to get together to talk and share secrets.

"Well, look at you," Jiggs drawled in her soft voice. "What are you all dressed up for?"

"Jiggs, you won't believe it," Charley burst out in an excited voice. "I met the most gorgeous guy when I was jogging on the beach this morning. He has dark curly hair, and his eyes are the color of the ocean. He has the cutest little dimple in his chin, and—well, on a scale of one to ten, he's definitely a twelve."

"A *twelve*?" Jiggs gasped incredulously. "Who is he?" she asked, running her hand through her curly brown hair.

"His name is Brett Murphy, and the best part is"—Charley took a deep breath and almost shouted—"he goes to our school!"

"No. That's impossible," Jiggs said, shaking her head emphatically.

"Why?" Charley spluttered.

"There are no twelves at this high school. I'm sure of that." Jiggs grinned impishly. "Being on constant boy watch, I'm sure I would have seen him."

Charley laughed. "Brett said he hasn't really started school yet. He said something about spending time with his coach."

"Wait a minute!" Jiggs interrupted, snapping her fingers. "He's not that famous diver, is he?"

Charley knit her brow. "I don't know. He didn't say what kind of coach it was, and he certainly didn't mention anything about being a diver."

Jiggs put her hands on her hips. "What's he supposed to say? 'Hi, I'm a star athlete.'" She shook her head impatiently. "Charley, you've got to quiz boys when you meet them. They just don't volunteer that kind of important information, you know."

Charley started to protest, but the bell rang, cutting off further discussion. They picked up their books and headed toward the big glass doors of Choctaw High. Just before she reached her classroom, Charley called out, "Remember keep an eye out for—"

"A twelve!" Jiggs finished for her. "How could I forget?"

Charley charged through the door of Mr. Tanner's homeroom and then suddenly screeched to a halt.

"My essay!" she cried, throwing herself against the wall in dismay. It was at home, now buried under the piles of clothes on her bed.

Chapter Two

When Charley walked into the dressing room of the Dalton Beach Ballet Academy that afternoon, the air was buzzing with excitement.

"He must be at least seventeen!" Julia Taylor said, carefully pinning her copper hair into a bun.

"I don't care how old he is," Marie Mathay said with a giggle. "What does he *look* like?" Her tight, curly hair bounced as she talked, and it always reminded Charley of the fur of a big, friendly poodle.

"Let's just say he's gorgeous!" Julia said as she applied some extra blush to her already perfect face.

Lindsey White pulled on an electric-pink leotard and added, "Well, it's about time some boys joined this class. I'm sick of just girls."

Julia was still looking in the mirror when she caught sight of Charley. "Did you hear the news?" she asked breathlessly. "A guy is joining our class."

"Great," Charley said, dropping her dance bag on the wooden bench and pulling out her tights and leotard. "Where is he?"

"I heard him talking to Miss Carabelli," Marie whispered. Then she suddenly burst out, "Oh, I can't stand the suspense! I'm going to go take a peek at him."

Charley laughed as Marie tiptoed out of the dressing room. Lindsey and a couple of other girls asked to borrow Julia's blush and then struggled for a position in front of the small mirror.

Charley slipped into her tights, scolding herself for bringing her rattiest pair. Even though she figured it was unlikely that she would meet two twelves in one day, she wished she looked better. But her tights had a huge run down the front, and her black leotard was shredded at the sleeves. One of her leg warmers had lost its elastic, and even her toe shoes were a little on the beat-up side. She pushed her frayed sleeves up toward her elbows and slipped an elastic around her tiny waist. All ballet students wore elastics around their waists to help their teachers see if they were holding their bodies correctly.

"Oh, Charley, he's Mr. Right!" Marie gasped, running back into the dressing room. She leaned dramatically against one of the benches and moaned. "Why didn't I start my diet last week? Why didn't I pay closer attention in class? I'm only a mediocre dancer, and he'll never notice me!"

"Don't worry. He'll notice you, all right," Julia teased.

"Wait a minute!" Marie said, suddenly standing up straighter. "Personality must count for something. I'll dazzle him with my charm," she said with a giggle.

"Just don't get near him on your turns," Charley said, teasing her. "Giving a guy a black eye isn't exactly a good way to make a great impression."

All the girls started giggling, and Marie put her hands on her hips, protesting. "Now wait just a second, please! I've gotten much better about that!"

When Marie had first joined the class, she'd had a habit of flailing her arms out on her turns, punching anyone within five feet of her by mistake.

"You're right," Julia agreed. "You haven't knocked anyone out in at least a month."

"Yeah." Charley giggled, reaching for her bobby pins. "I've even stopped wearing my helmet to class."

Charley had finished braiding her hair and was just pinning it at the base of her neck, when Marie swung at her playfully. Charley ducked and fell against Yvette Ferrand, who was quietly changing her clothes in the corner.

"Sorry, Yvette," Charley apologized. "Slugger Mathay is warming up for Mr. Right."

"That's OK," Yvette replied, a shy smile on her face.

"So, what are you going to do," Charley asked Marie. "Wrestle him to the ground?"

"You laugh now, Charley Maclaine, but just wait until you see him!" Marie sagged against the wall, one hand on her chest and the other fluttering in front of her face. "Be still, my heart!"

Charley started to kid Marie again, but she was interrupted by the sound of Miss Carabelli clapping her hands from inside the studio. She hastily tucked her pins in her hair and tugged on her sagging leg warmer. The rest of the girls lined up behind Charley, and they all paraded regally into the dance studio.

Charley took two steps into the room and suddenly froze in her tracks. Marie, who was trying to look poised and casual, crashed into her, and that set off a chain reaction, as Julia and the rest of the girls all plowed into them.

Cries of "Ouch" and "Watch where you're going" were followed by a stunned silence as they all gaped at the incredibly handsome guy who was talking to Miss Carabelli.

But the most stunned of all was Charley. There, not six feet from her, was Brett Murphy. He was wearing black tights with suspenders, a crisp white T-shirt, and ballet shoes. She couldn't believe her eyes. He was a dancer, and he hadn't told her!

"And these are my dainty ballerinas," Miss Carabelli announced in her clipped voice. "Girls, I would like to present Brett Murphy."

The girls giggled shyly as Brett smiled in their direction. His eyes widened as he saw Charley, and he gave her a small wave. She waved back. Catching a glimpse of herself in the mirror, she quickly tried to pull her right leg warmer back up and chastised herself for not borrowing some of Julia's makeup. The run in her tights looked even bigger than it had in the dressing room, and she vowed to buy a new pair as soon as possible.

As they all moved to the ballet barre, Brett came up to Charley. "I thought you might be here," he whispered.

Remembering their conversation on the beach, she whispered back, "Thanks for telling me you were a dancer."

He grinned and shrugged. Charley deliberately took a place at the ballet barre that was far away from him.

Their exchange hadn't gone unnoticed by the other girls. Marie, who had lined up behind Charley at the barre, whispered, "Do you know him?"

Charley nodded briskly. Marie giggled and remarked, "Lucky you!"

Miss Carabelli's salt-and-pepper hair was pulled tightly into a bun, and she was wearing her usual black leotard and knee-length dance skirt. Clapping her hands briskly, she started the warm-ups. "We will begin with pliés. First position, please!" Then she nodded for Mrs. Klein, the pianist, to begin.

The change in the class was remarkable. Everyone was on their best behavior as they went through their warm-ups at the barre.

The big mirrors that ran the length of the classroom were supposed to be used by the dancers to make sure their bodies were aligned and in proper form. That day, however, everyone was using them to spy on Brett.

Charley watched Marie's tormented face as she tried to raise her leg a little higher than usual. Julia, who was standing beside Brett, looked as if she were trying to perform *Swan Lake* single-handedly. Her arm floated around her head in flowery gestures, her best prima-ballerina look on her face.

Before Charley could sniff too self-righteously at how silly the others were being, she noticed that even she was working extra hard to keep her stomach in and hold her chin high.

The only person who didn't seem to be affected by Brett's presence was Yvette. She was working diligently in the corner, her brow furrowed in concentration as she performed the exercises.

As usual, in the second half of the class Miss Carabelli had them execute a series of steps across the floor. The dancers lined up in the corner and then, one at a time, took their turns.

The music was pounding, and so was Charley's heart. Leaps and turns were her strong point, but she suddenly felt as if she had never danced before. She could see Brett watching her out of the corner of her eye as she took her pose to begin. Charley chose a spot in the corner to stare at so she wouldn't get dizzy and then began spinning—four *pique* turns and an arabesque en pointe. As she spun quickly across the floor, she could feel her right leg warmer start to droop. When she got to the arabesque, it slipped completely over her toe, and she had to stop to tug it up.

Charley's face burned as Miss Carabelli stared at her. "Perhaps it is time to retire those," she commented archly. The girls all laughed, and Charley set her mouth in a determined smile as she finished off with the run, run, *leap* of a grand jeté.

As Marie began the sequence behind her, Charley yanked off her leg warmers and quickly tossed them under the barre. Then she returned to her position at the end of the line and tried to recapture her poise.

On the floor Marie was just finishing the combination. She was trying so hard to do well that she didn't notice how far across the floor she had gone. As she threw herself into the final leap, she crashed right into the wall with a loud *oomph*.

The girls all started to giggle, but Miss Carabelli immediately silenced them with a severe look. Marie sheepishly picked herself up and shuffled to her place in line.

It was Yvette's turn next, and she shot a frightened, imploring glance at Charley. Charley smiled and nodded encouragingly. For some reason, Yvette was shy about performing alone, and she frequently looked to Charley for support. It was kind of an unspoken agreement between the two girls; and after Charley's reassuring glance, Yvette's fright lessened, and she went through the steps without stumbling once.

Brett was the last one to go, and Charley held her breath, waiting for him to begin.

Brett executed his turns perfectly, and his leap was so high that the girls all gasped in delight and applauded. He smiled, looking slightly embarrassed at all the attention.

After class the girls huddled around him. "Brett, you're fantastic!" Julia cooed.

Marie bobbed her poodle hair up and down in agreement and asked, "Where did you study?"

"With the Dayton Ballet, in Ohio," he replied, draping a white towel around his neck. "But it's all still pretty new to me."

Charley didn't want to be part of the crowd vying for Brett's attention, so she deliberately kept her distance. She bent over to pick her leg warmers up from under the barre, pretending not to listen.

"My diving coach recommended that I try ballet two years ago," Brett continued.

At the mention of diving, Charley straightened up abruptly, banging her head on the barre.

Rubbing her head, she stared directly at Brett. *He's the diver Jiggs was talking about!*

Charley had momentarily forgotten about the mirrors, but she suddenly looked into one and realized that Brett was staring at her. As he caught her eye, he winked and flashed her a smile. Charley wanted to melt into the floor. For the first time in her life, she was tongue-tied. She couldn't think of one thing to say.

Charley shifted her gaze to the floor and headed for the dressing room to change her clothes. If she thought of something to say to Brett while she was getting dressed, maybe she could even catch him in the parking lot.

"Charley," Yvette asked, breaking into her thoughts, "could you help me with that last combination?"

"Uh, sure," Charley muttered as she struggled into her dress. The dressing room was packed with girls, all gushing about Brett. Charley waited for it to clear out, and then she went over the steps with Yvette as quickly as possible. Afterward, she grabbed her canvas bag and raced out to the parking lot, but it was too late. He was gone.

Charley couldn't wait to tell Jiggs about her afternoon. When she got home, she raced into the kitchen, reached into the refrigerator for the container of cottage cheese, and dialed the phone.

"Jiggs," Charley breathed excitedly when her friend answered the phone. "You won't believe what happened!"

"You got an A in Algebra II," Jiggs answered dryly.

"No," Charley replied with a laugh. "That would take a miracle."

"OK, then I give up," Jiggs said.

"Remember Brett—that guy I told you about?" Charley asked.

"The twelve?"

"Yes, the twelve. Well"—Charley took a deep breath—"he *is* the champion diver."

There was a loud crunching sound, and Jiggs mumbled, "That's terrific."

Charley heard another loud crunch from the other end of the line. "Jiggs, how dare you munch pizza in my ear!" she shouted.

"How did you know it was pizza?" Jiggs demanded.

"I'd know the sound of someone eating a double-cheese pizza with pepperoni on extra-thick crust anywhere!"

Jiggs stopped chewing, and there was a long pause. "You forgot the mushrooms," she finally said.

Charley took a bite of her cottage cheese and said, "Hear that?"

"No" Jiggs answered.

"That's because it's mushy, flavorless cottage cheese. The only thing good about it is that it's low-calorie."

Jiggs responded with another crunch. "I guess you could say you're suffering for your art," she mumbled.

"Suffering is right!" Charley said, looking disgustedly down at her dinner. Then she cried, "Oh, I almost forgot to tell you the best part."

"What?" Jiggs screamed back.

"Brett is in my ballet class!"

"You're kidding! That's great. Does he wear a tutu?" Jiggs asked wryly.

"Of course not," Charley snapped. "He wears tights, like everyone else. And he looks great in them."

"Hey, you guys could do *Swan Lake* in the pool and call it *Swan Dive!*" Jiggs joked.

"Get serious," Charley protested. "That's one of the dumbest jokes I've ever heard."

Jiggs stopped chuckling. "Sorry. I just can't believe that this guy is not only a champion diver and ballet dancer, but a twelve in looks as well." She lowered her voice. "I think you made the whole thing up."

"I did not!" Charlie protested. "The only problem is that he's a senior."

"So you won't see him in classes," Jiggs responded. "So what?"

"And when we're in dance class, we can't talk. And all the rest of the time—"

"He's at diving practice, right?"

"Right." Charley sighed.

Jiggs took a loud, crunchy bite of her pizza and mumbled, "Have you thought about getting together for breakfast?"

"I sleep late. And on the mornings I do get up early, I go jogging." Charley suddenly bolted up in her seat. "Jiggs, you're a genius!" she shouted.

"What'd I say?" Jiggs asked, mystified.

"Finish your pizza," Charley replied, laughing. "I'll see you tomorrow."

"What?" Jiggs shouted.

"Bye, Jiggs!" Charley called as she hung up the phone.

She smiled to herself as she carried the cottage-cheese container over to the garbage can and tossed it in. *He said he jogs early in the morning*, she thought, *so I'll just go jogging, too.*

Charley danced into the living room, chanting, "Neither snow nor rain nor burning sand can keep a woman from her man!"

"I think the word is heat, not sand," Mrs. Maclaine corrected, looking up from her crossword puzzle. She was curled up on the sofa with her feet propped up. "*And* I think they were talking about a postman and the mail."

"That's what's known as poetic license," Charley announced.

Her mom looked at her with a bemused expression as she danced toward the door. At the hall Charley turned and blew her a kiss before making a grand exit.

Chapter Three

At five o'clock the next morning Charley's alarm blasted shrilly in the darkness, and Charley nearly fell out of bed trying to turn it off. After flipping the switch, she squinted at the dial and flopped back on the pillow.

"Five o'clock," she moaned. "It's the middle of the night!" She started to drift back to sleep when she suddenly remembered why she had set the alarm so early.

"Brett!" Charley whispered hoarsely. She bolted out of bed and stubbed her toe on the dresser. Grabbing her foot in agony, Charley hopped around the room, stifling the urge to scream. Amanda was asleep in the bed across the room and she didn't want to wake her up.

Still only half-awake, Charley limped toward her closet to see if there was anything there she could wear that would get Brett's attention. Only a few dresses and skirts hung on the hangers, and they would never do for running on the beach. The rest of her clothes were scattered around the room on chairs or on top of her dresser. Everything was either dirty or wrinkled or both. It was depressing. She slumped on the edge of her bed and glumly surveyed the wreckage of her wardrobe.

Then her gaze shifted over to Amanda's closet, where everything was neatly organized and freshly ironed. Amanda even separated her hangers so that they were one inch apart. Charley sat up as something caught her eye.

That cute floral print top with the matching shorts would be perfect, she thought. It was so right, it practically had her name on it. And Charley knew the outfit would fit her because she and Amanda were almost the same size.

Then she frowned. Some sisters shared their clothes, but not Amanda. She was a real stickler about not letting Charley borrow anything.

Charley drummed her fingers on the bed-spread, looking at the closet, then at Amanda, and then back to the closet again.

Just this once, she reasoned silently. *Amanda will never know. I'll wear it on the beach and be back before she even wakes up.*

Ever so slowly, Charley got up off her bed and went over to Amanda's bed. Her sister was snoring softly with her arm flung over her face, so Charley very carefully tiptoed toward the closet and slowly reached for the hanger.

"Don't you dare!" Amanda announced in a muffled but stern voice.

Charley reeled away from the closet and stared wide-eyed at her sister. Amanda's eyes were still shut, and she was in the exact same position as before. It was hard to believe she had even woken up.

"Boy, that just burns me up," Charley muttered under her breath. Amanda had always had a sixth sense about her possessions. When they were kids, and Charley would try to borrow her bike without asking, Amanda could sense it somehow and would appear out of nowhere. Then she'd make a big deal of ordering Charley to get off the bike.

Charley checked the clock again and realized that she had to hurry if she wanted to be sure to meet Brett. After rummaging through the laundry basket for ages, she finally pulled out a pair of slightly wrinkled running shorts. Slipping them on, Charley decided to wear her olive-green sweatshirt. Then she ran a brush through her long brown hair, deciding to let it hang loose. As she ran along the beach, it would stream out behind her in the wind. *That will make a nice romantic effect,* she thought.

Just before she left the room, Charley walked over to her sister's bed and waved her hand in front of Amanda's face. Nothing—she was sound asleep.

When Charley stepped into the kitchen, her mother looked up with a startled expression.

"Charley, what on earth are you doing up so early?" she asked, setting her coffee cup down on the kitchen table. Charley's father was sitting beside her, listening to the morning fishing reports on the radio.

Charley had to think fast. She didn't want to tell them about Brett. Her dad would tease her unmercifully if he knew. She glanced around the room and spotted Brandy, happily munching away in front of his dog food bowl. With a triumphant look, she swooped toward him.

"I decided that Brandy just doesn't get enough exercise," she explained, a tone of concern in her voice. "Look at him," she added. "He's actually getting fat."

Brandy looked up at Charley. For a second he looked as if he understood her, then turned his attention back to his dog food.

"So, I'm taking him out jogging with me," Charley announced, grabbing the dog firmly by the collar.

"It was very thoughtful of you to put on makeup for Brandy's sake," Mr. Maclaine commented wryly, chuckling softly.

'Boy, Amanda wears makeup all the time, and you never even mention it," Charley complained. "But the one time I decide to wear a little mascara, you have to make a big deal out of it!"

"I think she looks lovely, Mac!" Charley's mother chided gently.

"So do I, Peg!" he agreed. "I just thought it was a little peculiar that Charlotte decided to get all dolled up just to go jogging."

"I am *not* all dolled up, Dad!" Charley protested, just a little too loudly. Her parents exchanged amused looks, and she felt her face start to turn red. She dragged Brandy away from his bowl toward the kitchen door.

As they stepped out onto the porch, Charley's father called after her, "Say hello to whoever he is for me!"

Charley turned around and gave her dad a surprised look, then stuck her tongue out at him through the screen door.

"What is it with this family?" Charley grumbled as they headed down the block. "They all know what I'm doing before I even do it."

She started jogging down the beach, then stopped to look back over her shoulder toward the white frame house. She half expected to see her mother and father and Amanda all following after her in matching jogging suits.

Charley sprinted down the beach, keeping her stomach held in tightly and her toes pointed. The wind was whipping through her hair, and she tried to imagine that she was one of those fashion models running in slow motion.

As she ran, however, there was no sign of Brett anywhere. She circled a couple of dunes, just in case he might be hiding behind one of them. Charley ran almost another quarter of a mile down the beach, but then she stopped abruptly. *This is ridiculous,* she thought. *He's not going to appear.*

Her hair was getting sticky and matted from the salt air, and she had an ache in her side from running too fast. She turned around and walked back toward her house, clutching her side. Yawning, Charley thought, *If I hurry, I can still get another hour's sleep.*

Just then her foot hit something soft and squishy. Charley screamed and tried to untangle the mass of seaweed from her ankle.

"Oh, *ick, ick, ick!*" she exclaimed. The seaweed was slimy and kept sticking to her toes and legs. Charley hopped around on one foot, trying to shake it off.

"I'll save you!" a male voice rang out. She stopped in midhop and watched as Brett bounced over and kicked sand at the seaweed. "Take that! And that! And that!" he shouted.

"Thank you," Charley said through her laughter. Then she folded her hands under her chin and jokingly added, "My hero!"

"Think nothing of it," Brett replied gallantly. Then, with his eyes twinkling, he added, "What was that, anyway—some kind of new dance step?"

"Yeah," Charley replied with a giggle. "It's called *The Dance of the Green Slime*. It's quite the rage." Suddenly she stopped and, putting her hands on her hips, said accusingly, "Speaking of dancing, why didn't you tell me you were a dancer?"

Brett smiled sheepishly. "I just couldn't find a good opportunity to bring it up."

"Right," Charley scolded playfully. "You just couldn't help letting me rattle on forever, explaining the most basic steps to you as though you'd never heard of them."

Brett laughed and shrugged helplessly. "Hey, I can always use a few pointers."

"You also didn't tell me you were a champion diver," Charley added.

"I'm trying to *become* a champion," he corrected, his face clouding for a second. Then brightening up again, he said, "You know, the diving coach here at Choctaw is world-class."

"You're kidding!" Charley exclaimed. She hadn't known that, and she secretly reminded herself that from then on, she'd become a diving fan.

Charley and Brett strolled along the edge of the surf for a while, the water coming just up to their feet. At times they had to scamper back out of the way when bigger waves rolled in and threatened to drench them. Suddenly Charley burst out laughing.

"What's so funny?" Brett asked, with a grin.

"I was just thinking. My one and only experience with diving competitions," Charley explained, "was at this Fourth of July celebration when I was ten. I'd entered the big diving contest at the city pool, and when my turn came, I announced that for my first dive, I'd be doing a jackknife."

"Had you ever done one before?" Brett asked.

"No, but I'd seen other people do them, and it looked easy enough," Charley answered. "Well, I bounced as high as I could on the board, reached down, touched my perfectly pointed toes—and then entered the water that way."

They both burst out laughing.

"I forgot to unfold," Charley said, giggling. "It turned out to be more of a pocketknife."

Brett chuckled. "That's happened to me, too."

"You're kidding!" Charley exclaimed.

"No," he insisted. "In fact, sometimes when I'm doing somersaults, I get confused and can't tell which is the sky and which is the water."

"You do?" Charley asked, trying to imagine getting that confused.

"Sure. They're both blue, and sometimes they blur together."

"Gee, I never thought about that," Charley mused. "Maybe they should dye the water pink," she suggested.

"Good idea," Brett said with a grin. Next time I compete, I'll mention that to the judges. And when the little men in the white coats try to cart me away in a straitjacket, you'd better say it was your idea!"

Just then a large wave broke around their ankles, and Charley leaped sideways to avoid it. She lost her balance and crashed right into Brett, who automatically put his arm around her for support.

She melted into him, her hand wrapping around his waist as though it were the most natural thing in the world. A thrill of electricity shot through her, and she looked up into his blue eyes. They were so warm and open. Her cheek brushed against his, and in that split second, she thought, *My head fits so perfectly under his chin.*

As soon as she had regained her balance, Charley sprang away from Brett and kicked at a piece of driftwood. By the time she had collected her thoughts, she realized they had begun jogging side by side through the water. Brandy loped alongside, and they ran quietly for a few minutes.

"This is where I have to run off," Brett said suddenly slowing down. "If I'm going to catch the bus to school, I'd better hurry."

"Wait!" Charley practically shouted as he started to leave. "I've got a car. I'll give you a ride, if you want."

"Gee, that'd be great!" Brett replied, his eyes lighting up. "My car's in the shop for a few days."

"I'll pick you up in forty-five minutes, OK?"

"Terrific!" he yelled, turning to run up the beach.

"Wait, Brett!" Charley cried. "Where do you live?"

He was almost over the dune when he turned and shouted, "Forty-five Pebble Beach Drive." He waved, then disappeared out of sight. Charley turned and sped home as fast as she could.

Chapter Four

Charley turned onto Pebble Beach Drive and slowed down, looking for Brett's house. Amanda was too busy applying her mascara to notice their change of route until Charley slammed on the brakes.

"Now look what you made me do," Amanda exclaimed angrily. "I've smeared my mascara." She turned to show Charley the black smudge that started near her nose and ran across her face.

"Sorry, Mandy," Charley said, trying to suppress a laugh.

Amanda looked around her and suddenly realized they weren't in front of the school.

"What are we doing here?" she asked as she licked her finger and tried to wipe the black smear away.

Charley beeped the horn. "I promised to give a friend a ride today," she said, trying to sound casual.

"*Charley!*" Amanda protested. "You know how I hate being late for school." Amanda testily dug into her purse and pulled out her compact. "First you make me leave early—I didn't even get a chance to finish my make-up—and now we have to haul one of your stupid little friends to school." She studied her face in the mirror and sighed loudly. "Why can't she take the bus like everyone else?"

Just then Brett walked out of his front door and trotted toward the car. Charley thought he was more handsome than ever in his pale blue polo shirt and khaki pants.

"Amanda," she whispered urgently, "lower your voice!"

"I don't care who hears me," Amanda grumbled, brushing a little blush onto her cheeks. "And I'm *not* giving up the front seat!"

"That's OK," Brett said, grinning at Charley. "I can sit in the back."

At the sound of Brett's voice, Amanda froze with her blush brush in midair. She slowly turned her head to face him.

Charley was mortified that he had overheard her sister. "Uh—Brett," she stammered, "this—this is my sister, Amanda."

"We've met," Amanda broke in sweetly, flashing him what Charley called her "killer smile." She didn't look fazed at all, either. "Brett and I are in a couple of classes together." She scooted forward to let him get in the car.

"That's right," Brett said, hopping into the backseat. Turning to Amanda, he said, "I didn't know you and Charley were sisters."

"By blood only!" she trilled with a twinkling laugh. "Other than that, we have absolutely nothing in common." She tossed her blond hair and added innocently, "She didn't even tell me we were picking you up."

Still smiling at Brett, Amanda subtly reached her hand across the front seat and gave Charley a strong pinch on the leg. Charley jumped, and the car lurched forward and stalled.

"You'll have to forgive Charley," Amanda said in a condescending voice. "She hasn't been driving for very long."

Charley shot her sister a withering glance and started the engine again.

"Take your time, Charley," Brett said, leaning forward. "I'm not very anxious to get to my European history class, anyway. History's always been my worst subject, and I hear Mr. Wade is a terror."

"Oh, he's just terrible," Amanda said, turning around and folding her arms across the seat to face him. "But I guess that's the price we pay for being seniors, isn't it?" She looked briefly over her shoulder at Charley. "You'll find out all about it one of these days," she said smugly.

Charley rolled her eyes as they turned onto Santa Rosa Boulevard. Amanda was only fourteen months older than Charley, but sometimes she acted as if it were fourteen years. She never missed a chance to rub their age difference in, either. Charley looked up and watched Brett's face in the rearview mirror. Finally she opened her mouth to speak, but Amanda's chatter started again before she could get the words out.

"I'm so surprised you know Charley. I wouldn't have expected you to have any time to meet people outside of class."

"Boy, that's the truth." Brett smiled ruefully. "Sometimes I think I spend my whole life in the swimming pool." He ran his hand through his dark hair and added, "It was a real tough decision to move here for the last quarter of my senior year. All my friends are back in Ohio. But it was my only chance to work with Choctaw's diving coach. And it took a lot of time and paperwork for a transfer so late in the year.

Charley smiled reassuringly at him in the mirror and then narrowed her eyes as she watched Amanda reach out a perfectly manicured hand to pat Brett's knee.

"Oh, you don't have to worry about a thing!" she purred. "After the big diving meet, *everyone* will want to be your friend."

"What diving meet?" Charley blurted out abruptly.

"Aw, it's nothing," Brett said. He edged forward with his elbows on his knees and looked at Charley in the mirror. "It'll be my first time out with my new coach, so it'll only be kind of a warm-up for me."

Charley turned her head and smiled. "Sort of like a dress rehearsal, huh?"

Brett laughed. "Yeah, you might say that."

"It's useless to try to talk to her about sports," Amanda snorted, shifting herself across the seat and blocking Charley's view. "Charley's too wrapped up in that ridiculous ballet."

Charley's eyes widened as she listened to her sister put her foot in her mouth.

"Why anyone would waste their time jumping around in those tiny shoes is beyond me."

Charley decided she had better stop Amanda before she made too much of a fool out of herself. At the stoplight by the school, she slammed on the brakes, sending Amanda flying clumsily against the dashboard.

"Charley!" Amanda screeched. "Watch what you're doing!"

"Sorry, Mandy. The brakes seem to be sticking a little bit." When she looked up and saw Brett grinning, a warm glow went through her.

"Drop us off right here!" Amanda ordered when they reached the school's front entrance. "Brett shouldn't have to ride to the parking lot. Besides, I want him to meet some of my friends."

"OK," Charley mumbled, her spirits sinking again.

Brett hopped out of the backseat and called, "Thanks for the ride."

"Sure," Charley answered. "Anytime." As she watched him stride up the walk toward the glass doors of Choctaw High, she suddenly got the awful feeling that once he met Amanda's crowd she'd never see him again.

As if he had heard her thoughts, Brett turned and looked at her with his incredible blue eyes. A slow smile crossed his face, and he called to her in an extra-loud voice, "See you at dance class, Charley!"

Amanda, who was still gathering up her notebooks and purse, stiffened. She just stood there with her jaw open, looking from Charley to Brett. She finally managed to smile, and then she very carefully leaned back inside the car.

"Why didn't you tell me he was in your ballet class?" she whispered between clenched teeth.

"You didn't ask," Charley replied, giving her sister her most innocent look. She waved jauntily and drove toward the parking lot.

Score one for me! Charley crowed to herself triumphantly.

At dance class that night, Charley stepped into the dressing room and did a double take. Every single girl was wearing her best leotard, and many of them looked brand-new.

"Oh, excuse me, I must be in the wrong place," she joked, starting to exit through the curtains.

"What do you mean?" Julia asked as she

tucked her copper hair high on her head with a lavender clip. Her shiny lavender leotard was cut dangerously low, and even worse, it looked terrific on her.

"Julia, is that you?" Charley dropped her bag on the floor and stepped back in shock.

"Well, of course it's her!" Marie said, lightly punching Charley on the arm. Marie had piled her curly hair on her head and tucked a sprig of baby's breath into the clip. Her leotard was a soft pink and matched her tights perfectly.

"Uh, Marie, you forgot something," Charley said, pointing to a price-tag string that was still hanging from her sleeve.

"Oops." Marie giggled, pulling at the string. "I just got it today," she added, blushing.

Charley put her hands on her hips and looked at her friends. "You guys look like a fashion show for dance wear!"

"Well, we don't want Brett to think we're a bunch of slobs," Marie mumbled through her teeth as she tried to bite the string off.

"I hope you're not planning to wear those awful tights again," Julia said, putting the finishing touches on her makeup. She wrinkled her nose, adding, "They have so many runs, they're practically obscene!"

"Don't worry. I finally decided to retire

those." Charley pulled a pair of black tights out of her canvas bag. "I've decided to wear these. They only have one small hole in them." Charley didn't want to admit to the other girls that after turning the house upside down trying to find something great to wear for Brett, they were the best she had been able to come up with.

Charley quickly got dressed and then carefully reached in her bag for her new toe shoes. She had stayed up late the night before to sew the ribbons on them. There was always something exciting about wearing a new pair of toe shoes, she thought, as she held one of the soft pink satin shoes up to her cheek.

"Hey, check out the dreamy look Charley's got on her face," Julia suddenly exclaimed.

"Oh," Lindsey White chimed in, "I see you decided to wear your new toe shoes for Brett!"

"That's not true!" Charley protested. "I just want to break these in for the spring concert." She felt her face flush, and she hastily slipped the shoes on her feet and tied the ribbons around her ankles.

At the mention of the concert, the girls all started talking about it. Marie, who had finally managed to bite the string off her sleeve, said, "All my relatives are coming down just to see me dance."

Julia smirked. "You call that dancing?"

"Listen, *Miss* Ballet," Marie retorted easily, putting one hand on her hip, "I come from a long line of klutzes. If I can get through the concert without tripping and falling on my face, it will be considered a major achievement in the Mathay family."

Just then Miss Carabelli clapped her hands, and the girls all filed into the studio. But Brett wasn't there, and they all turned to face the door, waiting for him to arrive.

"Girls, I would like you all to sit down for a moment, please," Miss Carabelli said. "I have a few announcements to make." They knelt on the floor, still watching the door. As if in answer to their expectant looks, Miss Carabelli explained, "Brett just called and told me he cannot take class today. He has to be at a diving practice instead."

A murmur of disappointment went around the room. "You mean I bought a whole new outfit, fixed my hair, and put on makeup for nothing?" Marie said in what she thought was a hushed voice.

"You look very nice, Marie," Miss Carabelli said soothingly. "In fact, you all do." There was an amused twinkle in Miss Carabelli's eye. "If you took as much time with your dancing as you do with your appearance, we just might have a ballet company," she added, before clearing her throat slightly and continuing.

"Now, as you know, the spring concert is less than a month away, and all the dances are in rather good shape. However," she added quickly, "there is always room for improvement." Miss Carabelli paced thoughtfully back and forth in front of her class. "Because Brett has joined our class, I have decided to make a change in the program."

Everyone sat up straight, their confusion mirrored on their faces.

"We will not be doing the *Bolero* piece. That dance will be moved to next fall's concert. Instead," she paused dramatically, "I will be adding the exquisite pas de deux from *Romeo and Juliet* to the program."

There was a collective gasp as every girl held her breath and stared wide-eyed at Miss Carabelli.

"I have decided to hold auditions for the role of Juliet. They will be next Saturday. We only have a short time, so I will teach everyone the dance today."

The girls all started talking at once and nudging one another. Miss Carabelli sat on the wooden folding chair and clapped her hands for their attention.

Finally everyone quieted down. "Partnering is so very different from dancing alone," she explained. "It is almost—how shall I put this—a conversation without words."

For a moment she looked up at the pictures of herself on the wall when she had been a ballerina, and her eyes shone. "To dance with someone is to move in complete harmony, responding to your partner's every touch."

The girls followed her gaze to the photos and listened with dreamy looks on their faces.

"There is nothing more exquisite than watching two people move as one. One body, one heart, one soul!"

As Miss Carabelli talked, her face softened and her long elegant fingers fluttered gracefully in response to her words.

She must have been beautiful when she was young, Charley thought.

"This pas de deux captures the moment when Romeo and Juliet first meet. It begins with the initial courtship." She spoke in a hushed tone. "They cannot take their eyes off each other. He is the most handsome boy she has ever seen."

Charley nodded unconsciously as she remembered seeing Brett on the beach for the first time.

"He falls madly in love with her immediately. But Juliet is shy, so she hesitates." Charley watched as Miss Carabelli seemed to become Juliet before their eyes. She tilted her head coquettishly and said, "It's her first grand party, and she is barely a woman. She dances in and out of his arms, first flirting coyly, then retreating timidly. Soon they delight in each other.

"Romeo dances his declaration of love for her. And then Juliet responds, dancing very shyly at first. By the end of their pas de deux, they fold naturally into each other's arms and, in purest innocence, discover love's first awakening."

Miss Carabelli folded her hands in her lap and let the love story hang in the air. Every girl in the room was imagining herself as Juliet. Charley could almost feel Brett's arms around her. They went through their warmups at the barre in a daze.

After that, Miss Carabelli taught them the dance, and there was suddenly a competitive electricity in the room. Everyone wanted to be Juliet.

After class Marie rushed up to Charley. "Oh, Charley, I'm so jealous of you. You're sure to get to do the dance with Brett."

Charley felt a tingle of hope go through her body, but then she shook her head. "Miss Carabelli is holding auditions, so that means any one of us could be chosen as Juliet."

"But everyone knows you're the best dancer in the school. She's only holding the auditions to make us all feel as if we have a chance at the part."

Charley grabbed Marie's hand and squeezed it excitedly. "I'd give anything to dance that part," she whispered.

Behind Marie, she could see Yvette going over the steps one more time. Her face looked so serious and thin—there was almost a birdlike fragility to Yvette. She saw Charley watching her and stopped, embarrassed.

"You were doing fine," Charley encouraged her. "You just left out one move, that's all."

Yvette tilted her head, and Charley came over to stand next to her, facing the mirror.

"There is a *développé* before the *pas de bourrée*." Charley demonstrated what she meant, rising en pointe and extending her leg high in front of her. She held it there for a second and then fell gracefully into a lunge and pulled her back leg into a quick three-step.

Yvette imitated her moves perfectly and then turned. "It always seems so simple when you do it, Charley. Thanks."

"Anytime," Charley said with a wave of her hand. Charley turned and practically skipped toward the dressing room.

She could hear Julia's voice coming from behind the curtains. "Charley's good at solos, *but*," she said pointedly, "Miss Carabelli said that partnering is a whole different ball game. Charley may not be the best at it."

Charley stepped into the dressing room, and Julia immediately stopped talking. There was an uncomfortable silence, and then Miss Carabelli stuck her head through the curtains.

"I forgot to tell you," she announced. "The boys from my intermediate class will be here on Thursday to run through the pas de deux with you before the audition, OK?" She smiled at the girls and added, "Good luck!"

Charley hummed a tune as she drove home

from the studio. Romeo and Juliet. Brett and Charley. She was already starting to fall for him in a big way. If only he felt the same about her, life would be perfect!

Chapter Five

By the time the last bell had finished ringing on Thursday, Charley was already at her locker. She spun the lock wheel deftly between her fingers, mumbling the combination numbers under her breath.

"Thirty-two right. *Ta-da!*" The battered hinges squeaked as she flung the door open with a dramatic flourish.

Books, worn toe shoes, notebooks, and old lunch bags slid onto the floor around her feet. Charley rummaged through the clutter, found her dance bag, and started shoving the rest of the junk back into her locker.

"Charley!" Jiggs cried. She was standing over her, wagging her finger disapprovingly.

"OK, OK, I'll clean it out tomorrow. I promise!" Charley protested feebly. She pushed her back against the bursting locker and slammed it shut.

"What are you talking about?" her friend exclaimed. "I'm not talking about your locker, I'm talking about ballet. You're not going to ballet class *today*, are you?"

"Jiggs," Charley said in confusion, "you know my schedule. Of course I'm going. What's so special about today, anyway?"

"Charley!" Jiggs rolled her eyes and looked up at the ceiling hopelessly. "Do I have to remember everything for you? Today's the *big meet!*" She stood there expectantly, waiting for the comprehending light to dawn in Charley's eyes.

Charley continued to stand there dumbly. "What meet?" she finally asked.

"The *diving* meet, you dope!"

"You're kidding! That's today?" Charley couldn't believe it. Why hadn't Amanda mentioned something about it to her? No wonder she hadn't run into Brett on the beach the past two days. He must have been practicing early.

"Oh, gosh, Jiggs," Charley wailed. "I don't know what to do!"

"Well, there's nothing to it," Jiggs said firmly. "You're going to the meet. You can go to ballet class any day."

"But Miss Carabelli hates it when we skip a class," Charley protested. "She'll be furious."

"Charley, get serious!" Jiggs put her hands on her hips and looked Charley squarely in the face. "Do you want this boy to notice you or not?" she demanded.

Just then Amanda came strolling around the corner, her regular quota of moon-faced boys trailing behind her. Her face was unusually animated, and she smiled happily at Charley. "Better hurry, little sister! You don't want to be late for ballet practice!" She turned to Skip Parker, who was fluttering by her side, and said, "Let's make sure we sit by the diving pool. I don't really care about all that swimming stuff."

That did it for Charley. No way was she going to let Amanda get the edge on her with Brett. She quickly reopened her locker and stuffed her ballet bag inside it. She turned to Jiggs with a determined look on her face.

"OK, buddy, let's go!"

The two girls took off down the hall and headed toward the gym.

The meet was well under way by the time Charley and Jiggs pushed their way onto the bleachers. The sharp bite of chlorine filled the air. A sprint had begun in the pool below them, and the crack of the starter's pistol made Charley jump involuntarily. Onlookers lined the swimming pool, and they cheered the swimmers on at every lap. Their coaches and teammates ran alongside, shouting encouragement in hoarse voices as they strained to be heard above the noise. Charley felt overwhelmed by the commotion. She didn't know what she'd expected a swim meet to be like, but the deafening noise was a real surprise.

The diving pool was off to one side and a little calmer, but occasionally a burst of cheering would spill over from the racers. Charley and Jiggs settled into their seats and tried to concentrate on the action below.

The rival divers were from Pensacola High, and one of them had just mounted the three-meter board. He paused a moment, then took three steps and catapulted into the air. At the top of his upward arc, he rotated gracefully onto his back and slipped into the water with a tiny splash.

"He's pretty good," Jiggs murmured to Charley as the audience applauded appreciatively. "But I bet he doesn't get a very high score. That wasn't a particularly difficult dive."

"It wasn't? It looked pretty hard to me," Charley started to say, but Jiggs cut her off, pointing toward the five judges who sat in a row across the pool. They each held clapboards with numbers on them, which they displayed to the crowd.

"See that?" Jiggs said. "All sixes and sevens. Solid, but nothing spectacular." Jiggs shifted in her seat and looked around her. "So where's this hunk you've been raving about all week?"

Charley craned her neck and tried to catch a glimpse of Brett. The Choctaw High divers were on a bench on the other side of the diving pool. They had their warm-up suits on and were huddled together, talking intently.

"There he is!" Charley blurted out, pulling her friend's arm excitedly. Jiggs's eyes followed Charley's pointing finger.

Slightly apart from the rest of the Choctaw team, a lone diver was limbering up. His leg rested on the bannister, and Charley recognized a dance warm-up they did in ballet school. Brett turned and walked back to the bench. His coach whispered something in his ear, and he nodded. Slipping off his warm-up suit, he strode toward the board.

"You weren't kidding!" Jiggs said, in a hushed whisper. "He really *is* a twelve!"

Charley hardly heard her friend as she sat there in shock. Brett was gorgeous. She knew from ballet class that he was well built, but there was something about seeing him in a bathing suit that took her breath away. A sudden giddiness came over her, and she gripped Jiggs's arm excitedly.

As Brett approached the diving board, the noise of the crowd fell to a subdued rumble. There was a sense of expectancy in the air. He mounted the steps, strode to the edge of the board, then turned and balanced over the water on the tips of his toes. Charley held her breath. Suddenly Brett leaped straight up and back, away from the board. He spun and twirled through a dazzling series of somersaults and twists like a flying fish, finally slipping into the water with hardly a ripple.

The crowd burst into applause as Brett popped up near the edge of the pool and lithely climbed out. Charley sprang to her feet and was clapping her hands for all she was worth, when Jiggs reached up and tugged her back into her seat.

"Let's see what the judges say first, OK?" she said, with a grin. Then she added, "But if you ask me, I'd say that dive was great!"

"Oh, Jiggs!" Charley gushed excitedly. "He's incredible, isn't he?"

Jiggs nodded her head emphatically. "He's good, Charley. Really good!"

A fresh burst of applause swept over the audience.

"Looks like the judges think so, too." Jiggs yelled over the noise. "Look at those scores!"

This time the clapboards showed four 9s and one 8.5.

Charley jumped to her feet, trembling with indignation

"What!" she shouted. "An eight-point-five! How could they? He should have gotten a—one hundred! It was a perfect dive!"

"Charley!" Jiggs's eyes danced with amusement as she pulled Charley back down beside her. "Charley, eight-point-five is a really good score. Besides, they throw out the top and bottom scores, and only keep the middle three, so the eight-point-five won't count. Brett didn't get any lower than a nine—and ten is perfection. No one ever gets a ten!"

Charley noticed that a few people were staring at her. She had gotten so wound-up that she didn't think about how silly she must have sounded, spouting off to the world on a sport about which she knew nothing. She gave Jiggs a chagrined look and shrank back in her seat.

"I guess I overreacted," she said with a shy grin. She looked back out at the diving pool. One of the other divers was preparing to make his next attempt. Once again, there was a hushed quiet as he collected himself on the board, then sprang into the air. His body was a blur as he spun through three forward somersaults before entering the water perfectly. Charley applauded along with the rest of the crowd. She had to admit that this Pensacola High diver was almost as good as Brett. One of the judges gave him a 9.5, but the average was the same as Brett's score. He walked calmly back to his bench and accepted the congratulations of his teammates matter-of-factly.

"Who is that guy?" Charley whispered to Jiggs. "He seems awfully cool about the whole thing."

"That's Scott Wren. He placed second in the state championships last year, and every-

one's expecting him to win it all this year."
Charley frowned, as she stared back at the
Pensacola High bench. Jiggs added, "Everyone on the diving team calls him The Ice-
man, because nothing ever seems to rattle
his concentration."

Some more divers from both teams went
through their paces, but Charley quickly saw
that Brett and the boy from Pensacola were
the two real stars. As she waited for the rota-
tion to get back to Brett, she pumped Jiggs
for more knowledge.

"Is it really true that no one's ever gotten a
ten?"

"Well, it's happened, but only a few times."
Jiggs cocked her head thoughtfully, then
said, "Greg Louganis is the only diver I
ever heard of who got a ten, and he did it
when he won the gold medal in the Olympics."

"Oh, yeah!" Charley burst in suddenly. "I
remember watching him. He was incredible.
I remember thinking that he moved like a
dancer, because he was so fluid and grace-
ful. . ."

"Charley," Jiggs cut in excitedly. "Greg
Louganis *is* a dancer! He's taken ballet all his
life." She slapped her head with her hand.
"How could I have forgotten that? He says his
dance training is what makes him great."

Charley blurted out, "I bet that's where Brett got the idea—"

"To take up ballet," Jiggs finished for her. They both laughed, then Jiggs looked quickly at the scoreboard, and her eyes widened.

"Charley," she gasped under her breath. "Brett is ahead of Scott Wren by seven points. If his next dive is as good as the last one, he'll win the meet."

Charley spun around in her seat and quickly looked over to the Choctaw High bench just in time. Brett's turn had come, and he was already climbing onto the diving board. This time there was no noise at all. Every eye was focused intently on Brett, and Charley could see that he was trying to channel all his concentration into the dive. He stood calmly at the back of the board, took a deep breath, then began his approach.

Just before he could leap off the end of the board, someone in the bleachers sneezed. Brett, obviously startled by the noise, didn't plant his left foot solidly enough, and it slipped as he tried to spring into the air. The arc of the dive seemed dangerously low, and Charley gasped in horror. The magic of the first dive had left him. He rolled forward with a single turn and entered the water quietly.

Charley sat there, stunned. "What happened?" she asked in a low voice. "How could a little sneeze distract him so much?"

"He must have choked," Jiggs said, shaking her head. Charley looked at her quizzically.

Jiggs shrugged. "It happens sometimes. Something happens that makes the diver lose his concentration." She patted Charley's arm sympathetically. "I'm sorry."

The scores were all in the low 5s, and Charley knew that Brett didn't have a chance to win then. She didn't even watch Scott Wren do his final dive; her eyes followed Brett as he walked glumly toward the locker room. His coach stopped him by the door and spoke to him intently, but Brett just stood there, shaking his head.

"Poor Brett!" Charley moaned. "Oh, he must feel just awful!" She watched him disappear into the showers, then turned to Jiggs. "I guess that's that," she said.

"Yep. That's that," Jiggs replied. They worked their way off the bleachers and out of the pool area without saying a word.

Even when they had reached their lockers, Charley still felt stunned. It was almost as if she had just lost a diving competition herself. She absently pulled open the steel door to her locker and yanked out her dance bag. Suddenly she froze.

"What's the matter?" Jiggs asked. "You didn't forget your purse at the pool, did you?"

"Worse!" Charley wailed. "Much worse. I just remembered why I had to go to dance class today!" She slammed the door shut and slumped miserably to the floor beside her locker. "This was the day the girls were going to practice partnering with the younger boys. It was my only chance to go through the dance for the spring concert with a guy before the auditions on Saturday."

"You're kidding!" Jiggs replied. "You didn't tell me that!"

"I know," Charley groaned, banging her head against the locker door. "I am so *dumb*. I completely forgot about it!"

Jiggs sat down cross-legged on the floor beside her.

"Do you know the routine?" she asked in a sympathetic tone.

"Sure I know it. I just haven't danced it with anyone yet."

"Well, then, I wouldn't worry about it too much," Jiggs said confidently. "You're easily the best dancer in the class. You shouldn't have any trouble with the audition at all."

Somehow Charley didn't feel convinced. "I don't know about that." Suddenly she burst out passionately, "If I don't get to dance the pas de deux with Brett, I—I don't know what I'm going to do. . . ." She trailed off miserably.

Jiggs put her arm around Charley's shoulder. "Hey, relax. It'll all work out." She hugged her friend warmly. "You're the best, right?"

"I'm the best," Charley repeated, laughing hollowly. "Right."

Chapter Six

Charley dragged the vacuum cleaner across her room, and the hose caught on the edge of Amanda's bed. She jerked it loose with a loud thunk and flicked on the switch. The vacuum came to life with a whining roar, and Amanda leaped straight out of bed.

"Charley! What in the world do you think you're doing?" Amanda screamed over the noise.

"What does it look like I'm doing?" Charley shouted back, vigorously raking the vacuum across the rug. "I'm cleaning!"

"At eight o'clock in the morning?" Amanda moaned, falling back on her bed. "On a Saturday?" She hurled her pillow at Charley. "Stop that racket this instant," she ordered. "I'm trying to sleep!"

Reluctantly, Charley shut off the vacuum cleaner and started stacking her *Dancemagazines* in a neat pile. Then she tucked her stray clothes back into the dresser drawers.

"What's come over you, anyway?" Amanda asked drowsily.

"*Fear!*" Charley shot back, hauling the vacuum cleaner out the door and toward the living room. She had tossed and turned all night and was still too agitated to sit still. Charley looked around restlessly for something else to do.

"Breakfast. I'll eat breakfast," she muttered, abandoning her cleaning and making a beeline for the kitchen.

Mrs. Maclaine was already sitting at the table in her fuzzy bathrobe, pouring her first cup of coffee.

"What are you doing up so early?" her mother asked as Charley dashed by her toward the refrigerator.

"Today's the big day," Charley replied, reaching into the crisper for half a grapefruit.

"Oh, that's right, the audition." Her mother

took a sip of coffee and asked, "Are you nervous?"

"Nervous? Mom, I'm paralyzed." Charley stared down at the slightly dried, unappetizing-looking grapefruit and grimaced. "Yuk!" she said, shoving it back into the refrigerator untouched.

"Now, Charley," her mother admonished, "you have to eat something. You're going to need your strength!"

"I'm going to need more than that," Charley joked half-heartedly as she headed for the shower.

All week long she had felt confident about the auditions, but that morning she didn't feel so sure of herself. Something was bothering her, and she couldn't concentrate. Charley looked out the window at the gray, overcast sky and thought, *It must just be the weather.*

At quarter of ten she tucked her brand-new tights into her canvas bag and smoothed her hair, which she'd pulled into a tight bun on her head and then lacquered with hair spray.

Her mom and dad and Amanda were all at the kitchen table eating breakfast when she crossed through the room, heading for the back door.

"Here comes our very own Juliet!" Mr. Maclaine called out.

"Charley, you look lovely, just like a ballerina," her mother cooed approvingly. Charley bowed in a sweeping curtsy and grinned at them.

"Your hem's coming out in the back," Amanda announced offhandedly, nibbling on a piece of bacon.

Charley made a face at her sister and retorted, "Thanks, but it doesn't matter. I'll be wearing a leotard and tights at the audition." She peered over her shoulder at the hem of her yellow cotton jumper and shrugged. "And, anyway, I just threw this on."

"It looks like it," Amanda said, haughtily arching one eyebrow.

Charley ignored her sister, and as she reached for the doorknob, her father proclaimed grandly, " 'Let he who has the steerage of your course direct your sail'!"

They all turned and stared at him.

"That's Shakespeare for 'good luck!' " he explained.

"Mac!" his wife said, nudging him. "You're supposed to say 'break a leg!' "

"I know, but that line is from *Romeo and*

Juliet," he said with a hurt look. "I thought it was appropriate."

They were still squabbling over the quote as Charley let the screen door slam closed behind her and hopped into her car.

When she arrived at the studio, Charley immediately saw Julia and Yvette, who were already dressed and going over the routine. She mentally kicked herself for not getting there earlier. Noticing that the order in which they would audition was posted on the bulletin board outside the dressing room, Charley went over and scanned the list. She was scheduled to go second to last, just after Marie.

Good, she thought. *I'll have time to practice.*

Just then Brett stepped out of the boys' dressing room and called to Charley. "Hi, stranger! Long time no see."

At the sound of his voice, Charley turned and almost gasped; she still couldn't get over the deep blue of his eyes.

"Hi," she replied, smiling. "Where've you been hiding?"

"Over at the pool, or here at the studio, learning the ballet."

"What?" Charley asked.

"Miss Carabelli has been teaching me the steps before school in the mornings."

"Oh," Charley said. "I guess that's why you weren't on the beach. I looked for you the last few mornings—" Charley's hand flew to her mouth. She hadn't meant to be so obvious. Casually, she added, "You know, while I was jogging."

He nodded. "Are you ready for the audition?"

"As ready as I'll ever be," Charley replied. Her stomach was churning with butterflies.

" 'O Romeo! Romeo!' " Maria sang out. " 'Wherefore art thou Romeo?' " She stuck her curly head through the door to the studio and motioned to Brett.

"Miss Carabelli wants to talk to you before the auditions," she said.

"Thanks, Marie. I'll be right there." Brett turned to face Charley and whispered, "Good luck!" Then he reached out and gently squeezed her hand. Charley felt her heart begin to race wildly, and she couldn't tell if it was her nerves or the warmth of his hand on hers.

At exactly eleven o'clock the auditions began. There was none of the usual dressing-room camaraderie, only nervous silence. One by one the girls entered the studio, and when each returned, the dressing room would go absolutely still as everyone waited for the latest's report.

The first three girls came back with slumped shoulders and looks of dismay on their faces that left no doubt as to how their auditions had gone. Then Julia took her turn, and when she returned to the dressing room, there was a triumphant look on her face. Charley saw it and began pacing anxiously in the corner. She could feel her muscles becoming tenser as her turn drew nearer.

After Julia it was Yvette's turn, and Charley gave her an encouraging smile. With her head held high, Yvette entered the studio. Soon the girls heard Mrs. Klein play the now-familiar music once again, and when it was over, everyone watched the curtains, waiting for Yvette's return. But instead, there was a long pause, and then the music started again.

"What do you suppose that means?" Marie asked in an anxious whisper.

"I don't know," Charley whispered back.

"It probably means that Yvette forgot the dance," Julia said in a catty tone. "Miss C's giving her another chance."

Finally the music ended, and Yvette burst through the curtains and into the dressing room. Her face was flushed, and her eyes shone with excitement. The others all stared at her expectantly.

"Well?" Marie finally blurted out.

"Well"—Yvette shrugged noncommittally—"I remembered the steps." Then she smiled shyly at Charley and added, "I think I did OK."

"That's really great, Yvette!" Charley tried to sound enthusiastic, but she was too nervous to really put her heart into her words.

"Wish me luck, everybody," Marie muttered as she walked stiffly toward the door. Moments later the music began again, and Charley tried to shake the tension out of her arms and legs. Then she rose up on her toe shoes and did a couple of *bourrées* around the room.

Concentrate! Charley ordered herself.

"I blew it!" Marie wailed as she crashed through the curtain, collapsing on her back on the floor. "My dancing days are finished. I'd better just hang up my tutu now! I'll never be Pavlova!" She raised herself up on her elbows. "A Baryshnikov, maybe."

That set everyone laughing, and Marie flopped back on the floor. "No, I can't even be him," she moaned. But Charley barely noticed Marie. Now it was her turn, and she took a deep breath before stepping lightly over Marie's body.

"Go get 'em, Charley," Marie said, giving her the thumbs-up sign from the floor. Charley squared her shoulders and stepped through the curtain.

Inside the studio, Brett was leaning easily against the ballet barre. Miss Carabelli was seated on her tall wooden chair, and Mrs. Klein was smiling up from the piano. Everything was the same as it always had been, but nothing seemed familiar. Charley shook her head, trying to get a grip on herself.

"We will begin now, yes," Miss Carabelli said, tapping her cane briskly on the floor.

Brett took his position behind Charley for the start of the pas de deux. He smiled at her in the mirror, placed his hand firmly on her waist, and waited for the music to begin.

Charley had practiced the dance a hundred times at home by herself, but it felt strange to be dancing it with a partner. She didn't have the freedom that she had had dancing alone. On top of it all, her feelings for Brett were getting in the way; she felt shy and jittery in his arms.

In the final lift she sprang in the air, and Brett shifted her onto his shoulder. But she was unsure of the move and nearly lost her balance. At the end Charley managed to eke out a confident smile, knowing that the finish of a dance was the most important part.

"Charley, what is wrong with you today?" Miss Carabelli asked sharply, her disappointment in her star pupil showing clearly on her face.

"I'm not sure," Charley replied, staring glumly down at the floor. "I guess I feel a little off."

"Well, never mind," Miss Carabelli said crisply. "We will try it again." She took Charley's chin in her hand and said firmly, "This time, work *with* your partner. He is there only to make you look beautiful! Remember that."

Charley blushed and took the starting position again, more determined than ever to get it right. As she did so, she silently screamed, *Why didn't I go to class on Thursday!*

Taking a deep breath, Charley nodded to let Mrs. Klein know she was ready to begin. That time the dance went better. She responded more easily to Brett's touch and even managed to add a few flourishes.

"Thank you, Charley," Miss Carabelli said curtly when they were finished.

Charley performed the obligatory curtsy and walked toward the dressing room in a daze.

"Well, how did you do?" Marie asked as she rushed to meet Charley at the curtain.

"I don't know," she answered with unfocused eyes. Charley was still going over the past few minutes in her mind. She walked toward one of the benches and sat down. "Fine, I guess," she added.

"Oh, come on," Julia chided. "Don't be modest."

"Yeah, you probably did great," Marie said, putting her hands on her hips.

Charley shrugged. The first time through she had been a little jittery, but the second time was much, much better. She felt her shoulders relax as she beamed confidently at Marie.

The next fifteen minutes felt like fifteen hours, but finally Miss Carabelli opened the door and called them back into the studio. They were too nervous to sit, and so the girls stood huddled together, waiting for the news.

"First of all," Miss Carabelli began, "I would like to say that every one of you danced beautifully. I am so proud. I only wish we had fifteen Bretts to go around. But sadly, we do not."

Miss Carabelli folded her hands calmly in front of her and continued. "As you know, the role of Juliet is a very special one, requiring a dancer with very rare inner beauty." She smiled ever so slightly, adding, "I am quite pleased with my choice."

Marie clutched Charley's hand and winked knowingly, while Lindsey reached over and nudged Charley with her elbow. Charley smiled modestly and waited to hear her name.

"Our Juliet for the spring concert will be danced by—"

Charley held her breath.

"Yvette Ferrand!"

There was a stunned silence. Then every single girl slowly turned and stared at Charley, waiting for her reaction. The smile on Charley's face froze, and she turned mechanically to look at Yvette. Her voice sounded unnaturally loud in her ears as she managed to say, "That's—that's wonderful, Yvette. Congratulations!"

Then the room became a blur to Charley as the girls rushed to congratulate Yvette. Charley could see Brett out of the corner of her eye, but she couldn't bring herself to look at him. Her throat suddenly ached, and her face burned with humiliation. She knew that if she didn't get out of there fast, she would make a total fool of herself.

Charley threw her shoulders back and, mustering every ounce of willpower she could, walked calmly toward the dressing room. There was a loud, angry roaring in her ears as she flung her dress over her leotard and groped for her dance bag. Then she charged for her car, praying she wouldn't run into Brett or any of the girls.

As Charley sped down Santa Rosa Boulevard, the wind whipped her hot tears across her face. Imagine losing to mousy little Yvette—of all people! Even losing to Julia would have been more bearable! She rubbed her eyes angrily, trying to keep her attention focused on the road. How could Miss Carabelli do that to her?

"It's just so unfair!" she cried out loud. At the stoplight, Charley leaned her head against the wheel and sobbed. All week long she had dreamed of Brett—of Brett holding her in his arms, of Brett lifting her gracefully above his head. She had imagined the roar of applause as she took her curtain call. Standing by her side, Brett would then offer his Juliet a huge bouquet of roses. She had even envisioned them becoming another Margot Fonteyn and

Rudolf Nureyev. And now, she felt like an idiot.

Charley raised her head and moaned. She would have to tell her parents, but she couldn't bear seeing their disappointed faces. And Amanda would never let her live it down. How could she face them?

Just then the light turned green, and Charley spun a U-turn, taking off toward the Olympia Stables.

"Jiggs!" she muttered desperately. "I've got to talk to Jiggs. She'll understand!"

Chapter Seven

Charley got out of her Volkswagen and walked with determined strides past the long line of stables. The air smelled like freshly cut hay, and she could hear the horses in their stalls. Off in the distance, Charley spotted Jiggs trotting around the riding ring on her quarter horse, Riley. Jiggs saw her at the same time. She stood up in her stirrups, waved, and then yelled, "Gee-yup, Riley!"

Charley couldn't help smiling as she watched Jiggs gallop toward her at full tilt. She looked like Annie Oakley as she waved her straw hat in the air.

"Whoa there, boy!" Jiggs pulled back on

the reins, and Riley thundered to a halt alongside the wooden fence. Then she swung her leg over the saddle horn, jumping easily down to the ground:

"Hi, Charley!" Jiggs shouted. "Boy, am I glad to see you!"

Charley nodded quickly in agreement as she felt her eyes start to well with tears again.

"I've got some great news!" Jiggs looped Riley's reins around a post and hopped up onto the fence.

"So do I!" Charley said, biting her lip. She wanted to blurt hers out, but something about Jiggs's face stopped her.

"I've just met a twelve of my own!" her friend exulted.

Charley looked confused.

"You know, a *twelve. Mr. Right*," Jiggs said, her eyes shining. "His name is Danny. He loves horses, he's taller than I am, and—" She clutched Charley's arm. "There he is!" she hissed, nodding toward the stable.

Charley looked over her shoulder and watched a tall, lanky boy in faded jeans, a work shirt, and cowboy boots stride toward them.

"He works here," Jiggs went on in a hurried whisper. "He just turned seventeen, and I think he's the most gorgeous guy I've ever laid eyes on." She looked at Charley expectantly and then turned back to face Danny. "Come on over here!" Jiggs called, her face lighting up. "I want you to meet someone."

"Sure thing, Janice!" he said in a friendly drawl.

Charley shot Jiggs a questioning look. "He calls me by my real name because he thinks it sounds better," she explained. Then she shrugged apologetically and laughed. "Well, I can't go around being called Jiggs all my life."

Danny took off his hat, and a lock of brown hair fell over his forehead.

"Danny, this is my best friend in the whole wide world," Jiggs gushed, pointing at Charley, "Charlotte Maclaine!"

Charley gaped at her friend, whose eyes were brimming with joy.

"Pleased to meet you!" Danny greeted her in a warm voice.

"Charley's a ballerina!" Jiggs added proudly.

"I might have guessed from the outfit," Danny said, grinning crookedly down at Charley's feet.

"Oh, my gosh!" Charley gasped. In her rush to get out of the dance studio, she'd forgotten to take off her toe shoes, and now her pretty pink satin slippers were covered with dirt.

"Charley, what's going on?" Jiggs asked, looking concerned.

Charley stared down at her ruined toe shoes and then back up at Jiggs and Danny. Right then was her chance to share her awful news, but she just couldn't.

Instead, she rose up delicately on her toes, her arms set in an oval in front of her.

"My big break could come any minute," she joked. "And I want to be ready for it!"

Jiggs and Danny laughed as Charley tiptoed in tiny steps through the dirt away from them.

"I've got to go, Jiggs." Charley waved a fluttering hand. "I feel a dance coming on!"

"Wait a minute, Charley," Jiggs called after her. "You didn't tell me your news!"

"It can wait!" Charley shouted, flashing her best smile. Then she turned and ran toward her car.

Later, when Charley threw open the back door, her mother was there waiting for her.

"Charley, where have you been?" she asked in a worried voice. "You've been getting calls from your friends all afternoon, and I didn't know where you'd gone."

"I stopped off at the stables," Charley replied. "I needed to talk to Jiggs."

"Well, Marie's called three times," her mother continued, picking up a yellow piece of paper that was on the table by the phone. "She sounded frantic and wanted you to call her the minute you came in the door. Julia called twice, and she said she'd try again later." Mrs. Maclaine paused. "Miss Carabelli called, too," she said softly, looking at Charley sympathetically.

She knows, Charley thought. She dropped her gaze to the floor, her cheeks burning with shame.

"Charley—" her mother began hesitantly.

Charley cut her off. "Thanks, Mom, but it's—I'm OK," she mumbled, taking the list from her mother. She knew that they all wanted to talk about the auditions, but she didn't feel up to talking just then.

"I think I'll wait a bit before I call them back," she said as she headed for her bedroom.

"Wait a minute, honey," Mrs. Maclaine said, in a hushed tone. "You have a visitor waiting for you in the living room."

Charley gave her mother a surprised look and slowly peeked around the corner. There, sitting nervously on the edge of the couch, was Yvette. Yvette was the last person in the world Charley wanted to see! She started to duck back into the kitchen, but Yvette saw her and stood up.

"Oh, Charley," she cried, her eyes huge and round in her white face. "I'm so sorry! I don't know what happened. Miss Carabelli must have felt sorry for me or something."

"That's not true," Charley replied in a mono-tone. "You got the part fair and square."

"But now that I have it, I don't think I can do it." Yvette's lip started to quiver. "Charley, I need your help."

"What!" Charley practically shouted. She couldn't believe what Yvette was saying.

"I know it's awful for me to ask you, but you've always been there to encourage me, and—and I just don't think I can do it alone!" Yvette collapsed on the couch and covered her face with her hands.

Charley's jaw dropped open. How in the world could Yvette have the nerve to ask her to do such a thing? It was bad enough not getting the part, but to have to help Yvette learn it and then stand in the wings and watch her dance with Brett? Forget it.

"You'll do fine," she said dully. "You got the part without my help, so you certainly don't need me now." Her voice sounded cold and distant as it rang in her ears.

It must have sounded that way to Yvette, too, because she looked up at Charley with a shocked, wounded look and then slowly rose to her feet.

"I do need you," she said quietly. "But I know how you must feel. I shouldn't have even asked." Her shoulders slumped as she walked toward the door. She put her hand on the doorknob, then turned around.

"Charley, you've always been a winner," Yvette said simply. "You'll have a lot more chances at the good parts because you're a beautiful dancer." Her brown eyes reached out across the room. "But this is probably my only chance to prove to my family and myself that I can actually dance well." She looked down at her feet and shrugged hopelessly. "Oh, well, Miss Carabelli will find out soon enough that my audition was just a fluke and that I'm not good." She opened the door and in a barely audible voice said, "Thanks, anyway." The door slipped quietly shut behind her.

Charley listened to Yvette's footsteps fade away as she went down the front walk and out onto the road. She waited to hear the sound of a car starting, but no noise disturbed the silence that had fallen upon the room.

She must have taken the bus all the way out here, Charley thought, feeling very guilty. *It must have taken all her courage to ask me for help.* But then Charley tossed her head defiantly. "Well, she had no right to do it."

Charley stormed into her bedroom and slammed the door. She was mad—mad at herself and mad at the whole world. Taking off her toe shoes, she raised them over her head and threw them as hard as she could against the far wall. Then with a sob, she flung herself on the bed.

Her stomach began to feel queasy, and Charley realized that she didn't like herself very much just then. She lay there for a long while with her eyes squeezed shut, trying to block out everything that had happened. But she couldn't shake one image from her mind—the image of Yvette standing forlornly by the door.

Suddenly she heard the familiar chug of *Peg o' My Heart*'s engines outside. Her father was coming back from a day of fishing.

"Daddy!" she said in a choked voice, wiping her eyes and sitting up. She quickly slipped her feet into her beat-up deck shoes and ran out to meet her father.

By the time Charley reached the landing, *Peg o' My Heart* was tied up at the dock. She stood back and watched the charter fishermen clamber onto the pier, clutching their catches of mackerel and pompano with self-conscious pride. They joked boisterously with one another as they posed for a group picture. Charley's father energetically directed the whole affair, waving an Instamatic camera like a baton.

"Now, Howard, you keep in back. We don't want to break the camera," he cracked. "I tell you, Fred," he remarked to a man in Bermuda shorts and a rumpled Hawaiian shirt. "I can't tell the difference between you and that red snapper you're holding." The man's face and arms glowed red with sunburn, and Mr. Maclaine added wickedly, "If you weren't the one wearing glasses, it'd be a toss-up!"

The men all laughed, then held their positions until the shutter clicked. Moments later the group broke apart, gathering their gear for the journey home.

"Hi, Daddy," Charley said quietly, slipping up beside her father once everyone had gone.

"Hey, how's my little girl?" he asked, looking down at her in surprise. Taking off his baseball cap, he slipped it over Charley's head, covering her eyes. Then he peered down with one eyebrow arched.

"Any good news for your old daddy?" he asked.

Charley felt her face start to burn with embarrassment and slid from beneath his arm.

"I'll go on down in the hold and start cleaning up, OK?" she mumbled.

A concerned look passed quickly over his face. Then he patted her arm gently and whispered, "I'll wind it up here and then help you finish up."

Grasping the rail, Charley swung onto the boat, flung open the hatch, and descended into the cool darkness of the hold. She flopped down by the empty ice chest and heaved a sigh of relief. The darkness of the boat seemed to quiet her turbulent thoughts. Maybe there she could figure out what to do.

After a short while she felt a little calmer. She started to tidy up, putting all the stray gear and tackle in its place.

"How about a cool, refreshing, caramel-flavored, carbonated beverage?" a voice drawled from above her head.

"A what?" she asked, looking up at her father.

"Most people call it a Coke," he answered. "But have you ever read the label?" He shook his head in disbelief. "Almost makes you want to stick to water." He held two cans above her head enticingly.

"Seriously," her father added with a smile, "I think a tall, cool one's in order, don't you?"

Charley grasped his outstretched hand and pulled herself up onto the deck. They took their Cokes and sat on the stern of the boat, dangling their feet in the cool water. For a while they shared a comfortable silence, each lazily taking sips of their sodas and watching the orange-red sun slip beneath the horizon far out over the Gulf. The water of the lagoon reflected the sunset like a mirror, and a pair of gulls chased each other across the sandbar by the channel.

Charley and her father sat there side by side for some time, and Charley suddenly wished desperately that time would stand still. She wanted to stay just the way she was right then forever—calm, secure, and protected.

As though on cue, however, her dad set his

soda can down on the deck beside him and looked at her expectantly.

"Daddy?" she said, taking a deep breath. "I—I didn't get the part. . . ." The words tumbled lamely out of her mouth and died in the still evening air.

"Well," he said slowly, "I kind of figured that might be it." He reached over, took her hand, and stared out to sea.

Charley stared at the calluses on his fingers, toughened from years of work, and the weathered skin of his knuckles. Her own delicate fingers seemed to disappear within the hugeness of his palm.

"What happened?" Mr. Maclaine asked gently.

In a confused torrent, the whole story came tumbling out of her—the disappointment and the humiliation and the unfairness of it all.

"And when Yvette came by to ask me to help her," she finished, shaking her head in frustration, "I didn't know what to say. I mean, at first, I thought, 'Of all the nerve.' " She picked at the tab on her Coke can. "But now I'm not so mad anymore. I don't know, it's just—well, I know I could help her. She's not a bad dancer at all, and with a little encouragement—because that's all she really needs—well

. . ." Her voice trailed off, and she looked earnestly up at her father.

He just sat there studying her face and waiting for her to continue.

"Why should I help her?" Charley muttered darkly. "What's in it for me, anyway? I've already lost my chance to play Juliet." Then she heard herself almost shout, "All right! I know I blew it."

Charley suddenly looked up, wide-eyed. There it was, out in the open at last. She hadn't done her best! She hadn't practiced enough, and she didn't deserve the part.

She turned toward her father, the pain etched plainly across her face. "I wasn't ready," she said in a tiny voice. "I guess I don't really have anyone to blame but myself."

Charley's father sat there quietly for a while. Then he slowly stood up and rubbed his neck wearily.

"I don't know about you," he rumbled, "but I could use another Coke. Come on into the wheelhouse." He stepped back onto the deck and headed toward the cabin.

Charley watched him in amazement. Hadn't her father been listening to a word she had said? A terrible disappointment enveloped her like a dark cloud as she got up and glumly followed her father into the cabin.

As she stepped through the door, her dad tossed her another can of Coke. Then he began rummaging through some receipts in a shoe box by the wheel. Charley stood in the doorway, waiting for him to say something and looking anxiously around her.

Her father had covered the walls of the cabin with framed photographs. They were everywhere, filling every nook and cranny. There were pictures of her parents on their wedding day, smiling brightly at the camera, and pictures of Amanda and Charley as babies in strollers and as little girls. There were Easter pictures of Charley and Amanda on the lawn in bright spring dresses, and a picture of Amanda waving from a float when she was homecoming queen. And there were pictures of Charley dancing.

Across the room, her father cleared his throat huskily. Charley looked up at him and realized he'd been watching her.

"Pretty good collection, huh?" He smiled crookedly. "Of course, I had about the best models a man could ever hope for." He pointed his can at one of the frames.

"Do you remember that?" he asked. "It was your first day at Miss Carabelli's ballet school."

Charley stared at the intense little girl in

the photograph who was clutching a pair of pink ballet shoes to her heart as though she'd never let them go. Charley smiled in spite of herself at the memory.

"That little girl wanted to dance so badly," he said, laughing gently. "You ate, drank, and slept ballet every minute of the day."

"I still do!" Charley laughed and sat down next to her father.

He pulled another picture off the wall, gazed at it a moment, then handed it to Charley.

"Now there's a day I'll never forget: your first recital. I thought we'd never get to the auditorium, we had to come back to the house so many times. First, you forgot your costume, and then your shoes—"

Charley broke in, "And then Mom found them in my dance bag. They'd been there the whole time!" They chuckled together warmly at the memory.

A strange feeling slowly came over Charley. Looking around quickly, she realized that most of the photos were of her. Every award, every recital, every great and wonderful moment she had spent dancing was preserved right there on the walls of *Peg o' My Heart*.

"You know, Charley," her dad said softly, "we all have disappointments in our lives from time to time, and they hurt. They really do." His voice cracked a little, and he gruffly cleared his throat.

"That's why this wall is here," he said, motioning to the pictures. "It gives me perspective on my life. Let's me see things in the long run."

Charley sat quietly in her chair for a moment. Mr. Maclaine stood up and hung the pictures back up on the wall.

"I've been pretty lucky, haven't I, Daddy?" Charley said softly. "I've gotten to do most of the things I wanted to, and I've always had you and Mom to help me out."

Charley's eyes brimmed with tears as she remembered all the nights her mother had stayed up late to finish sewing one of her costumes, all the times her father patiently watched her do her solo for the tenth time that day, applauding as loudly as if he'd just seen it for the first time.

"I guess I'm just about the luckiest girl in the whole world," she blurted out with a choked laugh. Charley jumped up and hugged her father for all she was worth.

"Now don't go getting all mushy on me!" he protested feebly as his strong arms held her tight. They started to laugh together, and

Charley knew then that she was going to be all right.

"So, what are you going to do?" Mr. Maclaine asked her, after a moment.

Charley looked up at him and said without hesitation, "I'm going to call Yvette!"

A broad smile slowly crossed his face, and he squeezed her shoulder. "I sort of thought you would!"

Chapter Eight

"Charley! Charley, wake up!" Mrs. Maclaine said urgently, shaking her daughter's shoulder.

"No, I can't go on," Charley mumbled sleepily. "I don't know the steps."

"Charlotte Maclaine!" her mother demanded. "What are you talking about?"

Charley opened her eyes and stared up at the blurry face of her mother peering down at her.

"Oh, I guess I was dreaming," she said groggily. "I was supposed to be dancing *Romeo and Juliet*, but I suddenly couldn't remember how it went, and no one would show me the steps. Then the ballet switched to *Sleeping Beauty*, and I couldn't wake up. I just stumbled around in my tutu, yawning and trying to open my eyes."

"It sounds like you were having the same nightmare all actors have from time to time," her mother remarked sympathetically. "Or maybe I should say all dancers."

Charley was finally beginning to wake up, and she squinted out the bedroom window at the morning sun. "What time is it?" she asked.

"It's almost noon, honey. Even Amanda has been up for ages. She left two hours ago."

"What day is it?" Charley murmured, confused.

"It's Sunday," Mrs. Maclaine said patiently. "Your name is Charlotte Maclaine, the next meal is lunch, and there's someone waiting in the kitchen for you."

"What?" Charley groaned, rolling over on her stomach. "It's not Yvette, is it?" Charley buried her head beneath the pillow. The night before she had agreed to start working with Yvette starting on Monday morning. The least Yvette could have done was give Charley until then to recuperate from the trauma of losing the part.

"No," her mother replied. "It most definitely

is *not* Yvette. I'd say your visitor is a little too brawny to be Yvette."

"Marie?" Charlie asked from under her pillow.

"No. Not unless Marie has dyed her hair, lowered her voice an octave, and had a dimple inserted in the middle of her chin."

"A *dimple!*" Charley screamed, ripping the pillow away from her head.

"Yes, a dimple!" her mother said with a laugh.

Charley threw the pillow on the floor and sat up. "Where is he?"

"He's in the kitchen talking to your father."

"Oh, no!" Charley screamed as she jumped out of bed and raced toward her closet. "How long has he been here? If I don't hurry, Dad will tell him all the stupid, goofy things I've ever done in my whole life!" Charley shot her mother a pleading look. "Mom, help me!"

"Now that's more like the Charley we know and love! You were asleep so long, we thought we'd lost you there for a while." Mrs. Maclaine smiled as she headed for her daughter's dresser.

"Oh, gosh, I don't have anything to wear. And look at me! My hair is a wreck!" Charley threw up her hands in defeat.

"Now calm down," her mother said, digging into the bottom drawer. "Brett said to tell you to put on your bathing suit and meet him downstairs in five minutes."

She handed Charley a sea-foam green tank suit and a pair of white shorts, and then walked out the door.

"I'll tell him you'll be right down," Charley's mother called from the hall.

Charley threw off her nightgown and yanked her bathing suit on. She rushed to look in the mirror over her dresser and grabbed her hairbrush. First, she brushed her hair into two pigtails.

"No," she muttered. "It looks too young."

Then she pulled it into a single ponytail in the back, but she quickly decided that style was too boring. After braiding her hair into a single braid down her back, she stepped back critically. It was too severe.

Finally, Charley shook her hair loose and let it fall around her shoulders.

"My hair will turn gray by the time I decide how to wear it," she muttered at her reflection. "This will have to do," she said finally, slapping the brush down on the dresser.

Charley pulled open the closet and looked at herself in the full-length mirror. She didn't look too bad: her suit was shiny and showed off all her curves, and the back was cut down to her waist and displayed her slightly freckled shoudlers. She slipped into the white shorts her mother had set out for her and headed into the kitchen.

But as she stepped into the kitchen, the ordeal of the day before flooded back into her mind. She was determined not to let Brett know that losing the part of Juliet had upset her. She swallowed hard and then pressed ahead.

"Hi, Brett!" she called gaily.

Brett stood up and grinned at her.

"Your father has been telling me about the time you caught the big sailfish and then cried when they wouldn't let you keep it in the bathtub."

"Thanks, Dad," Charley said, rolling her eyes skyward.

"Don't mention it," her dad teased back. She stuck her tongue out at him and grabbed a towel, but he was still grinning like a cat when she slammed the screen door shut behind her.

It was a warm Sunday afternoon, and the beach was already crowded with sunbathers.

Charley and Brett searched the white sand for a vacant spot. Finally, when they reached the last dune before the water, Brett held up his hand to indicate that they should stop.

"I thought you might want to go for a swim and then have a little brunch," he explained, holding up the little white bag he'd been carrying.

"Krispy Kreme doughnuts!" Charley squealed. "They're my absolute fave-rave! And"—her face fell—"strictly forbidden on my diet."

"Not these," Brett replied, grinning slyly. "I told them to take out all the calories."

Charley laughed and eyed the bag hungrily. She suddenly realized that she hadn't eaten anything since the day before. After talking to Yvette, she'd gone straight to her room.

"Maybe we should eat first," Brett whispered in a conspiratorial tone. "And then we can go for a swim."

"That's a great idea!" Charley nodded enthusiastically. "I'm ravenous."

As they sat down cross-legged in the sand, Charley was overcome by a case of the giggles.

"What's so funny?" Brett asked.

"I was just thinking about something my mom always says when we go out for dinner. Instead of saying she's 'ravenous' she always announces in a very loud voice, 'God, I'm ravishing!' "

Brett laughed and reached into the bag. "I like your parents," he said.

"Yeah, they're pretty great," Charley agreed, biting into a sugar-coated jelly doughnut. She smacked her lips happily. "Speaking of great, there is nothing more wonderful than a low-calorie doughnut."

For a while they just sat there eating and watching the waves break up on the shore. A warm breeze rustled through Charley's hair, and she turned to look at Brett. It was great that he had stopped by so unexpectedly, but it was almost too good to be true. She was a little nervous because he hadn't even mentioned the audition. She felt that she was waiting for the other shoe to drop, and it finally did.

"Listen, Charley," Brett said, sounding hesitant. "About the audition—"

"What about it?" Charley shot back, her doughnut suddenly sticking in her throat.

"I just wanted to say that I think you're a terrific dancer, and—well, if it had been my choice, I would have given you the part."

"Thanks," Charley said, trying to sound casual. Then she added with a strained laugh, "I guess you can't win them all."

She wanted to change the subject or make a joke out of it, but Brett's blue eyes were searching hers for the truth. In the end she decided to be honest.

"I don't know what was the matter with me yesterday," Charley said in a quiet voice. "I just couldn't concentrate."

"Those things happen," Brett replied sympathetically. "And when they do, you just have to tell yourself that it's not the end of the world."

"Sometimes it feels as if it is, though," Charley said, digging her heels into the warm sand.

"I know. You feel like a failure," Brett added. "As though you've let everyone down. But you've got to shake that feeling off and just keep going."

Charley knew Brett's words were meant to encourage her, but somehow she felt that he was saying them for himself, too.

"Sometimes I get so mad at myself," Charley finally added. "Not so much for losing, but for not doing my best."

"I know just what you mean," Brett said, nodding his head. "At our last diving meet, I really blew it because I wasn't trying hard enough."

"I didn't think it was so bad," Charley said earnestly.

"You were there?" Brett looked surprised.

Charley nodded. "And I thought your dives were fantastic."

"What about that last one?" he asked, raising an eyebrow.

"Well," Charley said, hedging, "it looked pretty good to me."

"That was *my* pocketknife," Brett admitted with an impish grin.

Charley laughed, feeling pleased that he had remembered her story.

They sat there, smiling at each other and shaking their heads. Then Brett scooped up a handful of sand and let it sift slowly through his fingers.

"You know, Charley, as long as we're talking about our failures"—he took a deep breath—"I might as well tell you—I have incredible stage fright."

"What?" Charley cried, floored. "But you seem so confident."

"Not really," he said, shaking his head. "That's the real reason I came here to train with Coach Morgan." Brett looked directly at her. "I'm fine in practice, but when I get up in front of a crowd of people, I freeze up!"

Charley stared at him with her mouth hanging open. It hadn't occurred to her that Brett might feel that way.

"That's why my coach asked me to perform in the spring concert at the ballet school," he explained. "So I'll get over my stage fright."

"It's funny how different people see things in different ways," Charley said, tilting her head to look up at him. "Performing is my favorite part of dancing."

"I wish I felt that way," Brett muttered, staring down at his hands.

A lock of his hair fell down on his forehead, making him look young and vulnerable. Charley wanted to give him a huge hug and tell him that everything would be fine.

"Well, I don't know if this will help with your diving," she began gently, "but the way I forget about my nerves is by picking out one person in the audience and dancing for him or her. Then the audience becomes a friend instead of a roomful of scary critics."

"Or, in my case," Brett added, "a panel of vicious judges."

"Right!" Charley grinned at him. "Have you ever noticed," she went on, "that in all the big ballets, someone steps forward and does this?" She raised her arms in an oval above her head and twirled her hands around each other.

"Yes, I have noticed that." Brett nodded. "But I never knew what it meant."

"It means 'Let's dance.' It's kind of like an invitation for the audience to join in."

"I'm glad they don't, or there wouldn't be enough room on the stage," Brett joked.

Charley giggled as she pictured an unsuspecting dancer giving the signal and suddenly being mobbed by the audience.

"Do you know what this means?" Brett asked, leaping to his feet and swinging first one arm and then the other over his head and then out in front of his body. Charley shook her head.

"It means 'Let's swim!' " He quickly threw off his T-shirt and raced toward the surf. "Last one in is a rotten egg!"

"Hey, wait a minute!" Charley called, wriggling out of her shorts. "You cheated."

Brett reached the water and dived into a wave. Charley was right behind him, and she shrieked with delight as the cold water splashed against her legs, nearly taking her breath away.

As they swam out into the Gulf, Charley marveled at how crazy everything had turned out to be! She had lost the part of Juliet, and she had lost her chance to dance with Brett, which she had wanted more than anything in the world. And, as if that weren't bad enough, she had agreed to help Yvette and to be content with just being one of the supporting dancers in the corps de ballet. But even so, she felt wonderful.

Chapter Nine

"Sixteen Palmetto Court," Charley muttered to herself, peering at the numbers on the little frame houses as she passed them.

She had promised Yvette that she would stop by that night to make rehearsal plans. The neighborhood was filled with small box-like houses that must have been pink and yellow and blue at one time, but the years in the sun had turned them all a nondescript gray.

"Ah, here it is!" she said, pulling up in front of a tiny white house with a neatly trimmed lawn. As Charley walked up the front walk, she stepped over a pair of roller skates and scooted around a big red tricycle.

When Charley rang the doorbell, she could hear two high voices arguing inside. "I'll get it!" one said. "No, let me!" the other argued.

A moment later Charley saw two little faces, smeared with ice cream, peeking out from behind the front door.

"Hi!" she said. "Is Yvette home?" She looked over their heads, into the living room. The television was on, and Charley could see an older woman moving around in the kitchen. The two little children solemnly nodded.

"Can I speak to her?" Charley asked with a smile.

They both looked at each other and then quickly slammed the door.

Surprised, Charley waited and was just about to ring the bell again, when the door was opened again, this time by the woman Charley had seen in the kitchen.

"I'm so sorry," the woman said with an apologetic smile. "You must be Charley. Yvette is expecting you."

"Mrs. Ferrand?" Charley asked, studying the woman's face. She nodded, and Charley realized that she wasn't as old as she had looked at first. She must have been a little tired.

The two little children suddenly peeked out

from behind their mother's skirt. "Mommy, Yvette's in her studio," one of them whispered.

Mrs. Ferrand absentmindedly patted the little girl on the head and stepped out on the porch.

"What she really means is the garage," Mrs. Ferrand explained. "It's around back—just follow the driveway."

Charley nodded and walked around to the back of the house. A light was shining through the garage window, and Charley could hear Tchaikovsky's "Waltz of the Flowers" crackling on a record player.

She tiptoed up to the window and peered in. There stood Yvette, clad in her leotard and tights, wearing her toe shoes. She was repeating a combination they had done in class the week before. In class she had been hesitant and had even forgotten the steps. Alone in her garage, however, she was perfect.

Charley couldn't get over the change. She watched Yvette do an arabesque en pointe with her leg extended up straight behind her. She stood perfectly still with her head held high, then gracefully passed her leg in front of her and bourréed forward. Every movement was clean and strong and elegant.

Charley held her breath as Yvette prepared

for a pirouette. "One, two, *three* turns," Charley gasped as she counted out loud. Then she found herself applauding the perfectly executed pirouette.

"Charley, is that you?" Yvette called out, hearing the clapping. She walked over to the record player and lifted the needle. "Charley?" she called again nervously.

"Yvette, you were wonderful!" Charley called, as she burst through the side door.

"You were watching me?" Yvette asked shyly.

"Yes, and you're great!" Charley replied. "Why don't you dance that way in class?"

Yvette just shook her head and nervously brushed a stray lock of hair from her forehead.

"Come on, Yvette, this is exciting," Charley went on eagerly. "I mean, when you asked me for help I was"—Charley shrugged—"well, I was afraid that the best we would be able to do was make sure you got the steps right. But—" Charley's hand flew to her mouth, and her eyes opened wide. "Me and my motor mouth! I didn't mean to say that. I mean—"

"It's OK," Yvette said, looking at the floor.

"What I meant to say is that you really are good." Charley leaned forward and looked at Yvette earnestly. "It seems to me that you just need a little confidence, that's all."

"Thanks, Charley." Yvette beamed. "That means a lot, coming from you."

Charley smiled and looked around the room curiously, noticing it for the first time. "Is this your studio?" she asked.

"Late at night it is. During the mornings and afternoons, my mom runs a day-care center here."

Yvette pointed to the brightly colored boxes that held stuffed animals and dolls. "My mom and I look after some of the neighbors' kids until their parents get home from work."

"You do that before you go to class?" Charley asked.

"Umm-hmm." Yvette nodded, slipping a puppet onto her hand. "And on Saturday mornings," she said in a high-pitched voice as she maneuvered the puppet, "I teach them all ballet lessons."

"Wow!" Charley said, leaning against the makeshift dance barre. "I'm really impressed."

"Well, it helps pay for my dance classes," Yvette explained, returning to her normal voice. She tucked the puppet back into the toy box.

Charley grinned at Yvette. At first she had felt sorry for the other girl, but now she realized that there was much more to Yvette than met the eye. She was courageous and hard-working, and she just needed a little more self-esteem to really come into her own. Charley knew she could help Yvette find it.

"So!" Charley said, clapping her hands together and imitating Miss Carabelli. "This week, Miss C. will teach you the pas de deux, and then we can begin fine-tuning next week, yes?"

Yvette made a sweeping curtsy and answered in her most appreciative voice, "I am so very grateful!"

Charley laughed and curtsied back. Then she said, "Boy, I can't wait until the others see you. You're going to knock their socks off."

"Oh, Charley, please don't tell them you're helping me!" Yvette pleaded. She suddenly looked panicked. "They already think I don't deserve the part, and—well, if they knew, I'd never live it down."

"Sure," Charley replied with a shrug. "We can keep it a secret if you want."

"I'd really appreciate it," Yvette said, sounding a little more calm.

"Hmm," Charley said. "It's awfully hard to keep things from Julia and Marie. They're both such busybodies."

"How about if we work in the mornings before school?" Yvette suggested.

"That will help," Charley agreed. "But we need a surefire way to disguise what we're doing, so they'll never even suspect."

Charley paced in a circle around Yvette. Then, she stopped and snapped her fingers. "I've got an idea!" she burst out. She rushed over to Yvette and shook her by the shoulder. "And it's brilliant!"

A week later Miss Carabelli dismissed her Monday afternoon class promptly at six o'clock. Brett disappeared into the men's dressing room, and Mrs. Klein gathered up her sheet music and left the studio with Miss Carabelli. The girls all chattered away as they quickly gathered their leg warmers and bags from beneath the barre and under the piano.

At the studio door, Yvette accidentally jostled Charley with her elbow.

"Why don't you watch where you're going?" Charley hissed angrily.

"Look, you were the one who ran into me," Yvette replied boldly. "You should apologize."

Julia and Marie, who were about to go through the door, turned and stared at them with open mouths.

"Just because you're playing Juliet doesn't mean you own the whole studio," Charley shouted. "Because you don't!"

"Look who's talking!" Yvette snapped back.

"Hey, come on, Charley!" Marie exclaimed, stepping between them. "Calm down, OK? It wasn't anybody's fault."

Charley and Yvette both glared at Marie.

"This is between the two of us," Charley said meaningfully. "So just butt out!"

"OK, OK," Marie said, her hands held up in front of her. She grabbed Julia, and they retreated into the dressing room, pulling the studio door shut behind them.

Charley and Yvette stood there silently, staring at each other. Then they broke into gales of laughter.

"*Shhh!*" Charley whispered, trying to control her giggles. "They might come back and find out that this was all a joke!"

"Can you believe the look on Julia's face?" Yvette whispered.

"Even Marie was speechless," Charley added, putting her arm around Yvette. "And *that's* a first. Oh, I wish I could be a bug on the wall of the dressing room right now. They're probably all talking about us, and if I know Julia and Marie, they'll be on the phone all night telling anyone who'll listen that you and I are archenemies and that I've turned into a spoilsport."

"Oh, Charley, I don't want that to happen!" Yvette said with a concerned look on her face.

"Don't worry," Charley replied. "It's the best way to keep them from guessing that we're working together, and it's only for a few more weeks. Besides, now that they think I'm being a jerk, they'll be behind you one hundred percent. Then, after they've seen what a terrific Juliet you are, we can tell them it was all a joke and have a big laugh about it."

"I hope you're right," Yvette said in an unsteady voice.

"Of course I'm right," Charley replied with confidence. Then she snapped her fingers. "Oh, did you remember to ask Miss Carabelli if we could use the studio in the morning?"

Yvette nodded. "And I made sure she thought I would be working alone."

"Good," Charley said with a sure smile. "So, we'll meet here before school tomorrow."

Yvette started to respond, but Charley suddenly put her finger to her lips. Then she slowly tiptoed over and put her ear against the door.

"I'll bet somebody's listening to us," Charley mouthed to Yvette. Then she said in an extra-loud voice, "Yvette Ferrand, I don't care if I ever talk to you again."

When she flung open the studio door a moment later, Julia, Marie, and Lindsey nearly fell onto the floor. They had changed into their street clothes and had their dance bags over their shoulders.

"Uh, we just wanted to know if you need a ride home, Yvette," Julia said, breezing past Charley and into the studio.

"Yeah," Lindsey added with a toss of her head. "I'm driving."

Even Marie gave Charley the cold shoulder as she marched past her to stand by Yvette.

Behind them, Charley winked at Yvette and gave her a triumphant I-told-you-so look. Then she rushed into the dressing room to change her clothes. A moment later Yvette came in, threw her jumper over her head, grabbed her shoes, and turned back toward the studio. Just before she slipped out the door, she looked at Charley and winked.

Charley was still laughing to herself as she slipped on a pair of jeans and a pink pullover. Their plan had worked even better than she'd expected!

As Charley skipped into the parking lot,

she recognized a familiar figure leaning against her car, silhouetted against the evening sky.

"Brett!" she sang out, thrilled that he had waited for her. She quickly pulled the pins out of her hair and let it hang in a shiny ponytail.

"I didn't expect to see you here," she said brightly when she came up to him. Usually he dressed quickly and went straight home.

"I wanted to talk to you," Brett said gruffly, kicking at the ground.

"What about?" Charley asked in a hesitant voice. There was something about the tone of his voice that made her smile disappear.

"Well, I couldn't help overhearing your argument with Yvette after class." He raised his head and looked directly at her. "And I don't understand why you're acting this way."

"Oh, *that!*" Charley laughed, feeling relieved. "It's just a jo—" She stopped, remembering she had promised Yvette she would keep their secret. That meant not telling anyone—not even Brett.

"It's just between me and Yvette," she muttered. Then she bit her lip and added in a bright tone, "Well, it'll all work out."

"I hope it does," Brett agreed, concern darkening his eyes. "Because I'd hate to see you get as competitive as some of the people I've danced with. It can be really destructive."

His face was so earnest and anxious that Charley wanted to be able to laugh and let him know that everything was really fine. But she couldn't, so she just nodded and stared at the ground.

"So, will I see you on the beach tomorrow?" he asked, changing the subject.

"Sure," Charley responded in a cheery voice. "I'll be there bright and early." Then her shoulders slumped as she remembered she had to rehearse with Yvette. "Oh, wait a minute. I can't meet you tomorrow morning."

"Well," he said with a smile, "Wednesday, then?"

"I can't see you Wednesday, either, Brett," Charley said miserably. "In fact, I won't be able to see you at all for a while."

"Why?" Brett asked, looking confused.

Charley took a deep breath and said lamely, "I can't tell you."

"Oh. Well, I understand," Brett replied in a brusque voice. "Maybe we can get together at school, then."

He tried to look nonchalant, but Charley could tell he thought she was brushing him off.

"See you around," he said, waving slightly. Then he jammed his hands in his pockets and walked slowly toward his car.

"Bye, Brett," she whispered. Every part of her body wanted to call him back or run after him and explain it all. But she didn't move. Instead she watched helplessly as he started his car and drove off down the road.

"Me and my big ideas!" Charley fumed, angrily kicking the tire of her car. Her funny secret didn't seem so funny anymore. No, it had suddenly become a heavy weight, and her chest ached already from trying to hold it in.

Two days later the phone rang, and Charley rushed to get it, hoping it would be Brett.

"All right, Charley!" a familiar voice demanded from the other end of the line. "What's going on?"

"Hi, Jiggs!" Charley answered. "What do you mean, 'What's going on?' "

"I don't see you before school anymore, when we pass in the halls, you look right through me, *and* worst of all, you're starting to get that haunted, sickly look of yours. That can mean only one of two things: Either you've started another one of your killer diets, or something is bothering you."

"I'm not on a diet," Charley responded carefully.

There was a long silence from the other end of the line, and finally Jiggs asked in a meek voice, "Is it something I did?"

"Of course not!" Charley quickly assured her.

"Then what is it?" Jiggs persisted.

"I can't tell you."

"What do you mean, you can't tell me?" Jiggs exploded. "This is me, remember—your very best friend in the whole wide world. We tell each other everything."

"I can't say anything because I've been sworn to secrecy."

"By whom?"

"If I told you that, it would give away the secret."

"OK," Jiggs said finally. "How about a hint?" she asked after a short pause.

"I can't," Charley said, shaking her head. "Really."

"Just the initials?" Jiggs prodded.

"Jiggs!" Charley said firmly. "I said I can't."

"Boy, you're tough."

"Let's talk about something else," Charley quickly suggested. "How's Danny, anyway?"

"Danny's great!" Jiggs answered happily. "How's your twelve?"

"He's still a twelve," Charley replied in a dull tone. "But our relationship has turned into a big zero."

"Oh, Charley, that's awful!" Jiggs's voice was filled with concern. "What happened?"

This time it was Charley's turn to pause. She wanted to tell Jiggs all about it, but her secret stood in the way. "I can't talk about it," she finally replied.

There was another unbearably long pause, and finally Jiggs spoke. "Well, when you can talk about something, give me a call." Her voice suddenly sounded distant. "Or maybe we can even say 'hi' in the halls once in a while," she suggested. "I, uh, guess I'll see you."

"Oh, Jiggs!" Charley wailed.

"Bye, Charley," Jiggs said. Then she hung up.

Charley listened to the dial tone buzzing in her ear, deciding it was a horribly lonely sound. She slowly placed the receiver back on its cradle and stood there staring off into space.

"Is something wrong?" her mother asked as she went into the kitchen.

"No!" Charley said with an exaggerated laugh. "Everything's *terrific*! The girls in my dance class think I'm public enemy number one, my best friend thinks I've deserted her, and the only boy I've ever really cared for is ignoring me. Things couldn't be better!"

Chapter Ten

On Thursday morning Charley dragged herself out of bed and headed for the laundry basket. She grabbed the first thing she could find and threw it on. Then she dug into her dresser and pulled out her oldest leotard. It had been black at one time but had faded to a murky gray. She slipped her feet into a pair of sandals and slouched toward the kitchen.

"Well, look what the cat dragged in!" Amanda chirped.

Charley looked up and couldn't believe her eyes. Her sister was wearing pink satin jogging shorts, along with a lavender-and-pink matching top. She was even wearing a headband that had tiny pink-and-purple stripes.

"Amanda," Charley practically croaked, "what are you doing up so early?"

"What does it look like?" Amanda said, bending over in a halfhearted attempt to touch her toes. "I'm going jogging, of course!"

"But you've never exercised in your entire life!" Charley reminded her.

"Well, now's as good a time to start as any," Amanda announced smugly. She jogged in a circle around Charley and then sailed out the back door.

"I'll tell Brett you said hi!" she called over her shoulder.

"Brett!" Charley screamed after her, closing the screen door with a bang. She turned around and saw her mother and father, coffee cups in hand, gaping at her. They'd witnessed the entire scene.

"I thought Brett was *your* friend," Mrs. Maclaine remarked, looking perplexed.

" 'Was' is right," Charley answered dejectedly. She toasted a piece of bread and then covered it with peanut butter and jelly.

"Well, at least your appetite has improved," her mother noted with a smile.

"Yeah, my appetite is great," Charley said.

"But my social life is a big zero!" Taking a huge bite of toast, she mumbled, "I'm going to be the healthiest wallflower in town."

After the morning's practice with Yvette two days before the dance concert, Charley drove to school, running through the events of the past few weeks in her head. There was no doubt about it—her plan had worked too well. The girls in Miss Carabelli's dance class were actively shunning her, Brett hardly looked at her anymore, and now Amanda was even moving in on him. Things had never looked so bleak. There was only one thing Charley could think of to do—secret or no secret, she had to tell Jiggs. Charley had to get it all out before the pressure made her burst.

During Mr. Phelps's first-period English class, she scribbled out a note:

Jiggs,
   I've got to see you!!! Meet me in the usual place fifteen minutes after second period begins.
DESPERATELY yours, C.M.

As she folded the note, Mr. Phelps walked by Charley's desk and almost caught her in the act. Thinking fast, she deliberately picked up her pen and wrote "Thoughts About Long-fellow" on the outside in big letters. Mr. Phelps smiled at her approvingly and then continued down the aisle.

When the bell rang, Charley raced over to Jiggs's locker. She knew her friend would go there to get her second-period books, so Charley stuffed the note in between the locker's metal frame and the door. She would have waited for Jiggs, but her Algebra II class was at the far end of the school, and she needed a few minutes to plan her excuse to get out of class.

Charley turned down the corridor toward her class and nearly bumped into Amanda and Brett. Amanda was leaning against the wall clutching her notebook to her chest and looking dreamily into Brett's eyes. Brett was doing all the talking, gesturing emphatically with one hand. The other hand was propped against the wall over Amanda's head. They looked very cozy.

Luckily neither of them saw Charley, and she kept her gaze focused straight ahead and charged into class. By the time she was seated at her desk, she was seeing red. The vision of them together was emblazoned in her mind.

Charley stared wild eyed into space, clenching and unclenching her jaw.

"Charlotte Maclaine, did you hear what I asked you?" Miss Cody, the algebra teacher, called from the front of the classroom.

Charley suddenly realized that all the students in the class had turned in their seats and were staring at her. Her face suddenly felt white hot, and she said, "I'm sorry, Miss Cody. Could you repeat the question?"

"I asked you if you were feeling well?"

"I'm fine," Charley said, starting to slink down behind her desk. Then she caught a glimpse of the clock and bolted up again. "*No!* I feel awful!" she shouted. It was exactly a quarter after the hour, and she had a meeting with Jiggs.

"I thought you looked rather pale," Miss Cody said. "Here, let me give you a pass. I want you to go straight to the nurse's office."

Charley started to jump up from her desk but remembered just in time that she was supposed to look ill. She put her hand to her forehead and buckled her knees. Then, with small, halting steps, she staggered to the front of the room and started out of the classroom.

She turned, clinging to the door, and said weakly, "Thank you, Miss Cody." As soon as she was out of sight of the classroom, she bolted down the hall.

"Hall pass, please!" a pudgy boy with glasses ordered from a chair by the cafeteria. Charley stopped and handed it to him, impatiently checking her watch. She was already five minutes late, and Jiggs might give up, thinking she couldn't get out of class. She nervously tapped her foot waiting for the boy to let her leave. He took his time, carefully writing her name and the time down in his notebook. Then he methodically folded the pass.

"Where are you going?" he asked suspiciously.

"The nurse's office," Charley said, remembering she was supposed to look ill. She clutched her stomach and let out a groan.

"OK. Here's your pass," he said, quickly handing it back to her. He looked as if he thought she might get sick all over him.

Charley suppressed a giggle as she limped down the hall toward the place where she always met Jiggs. When she got there, she looked both ways, then knocked on the door three times.

"Who is it?" Jiggs asked loudly.

"It's me!" Charley whispered.

The wooden door creaked open slowly, and

a long, thin hand reached out and grabbed Charley by the elbow, yanking her inside. The door shut quickly behind her, and Charley was suddenly engulfed by darkness.

"You did *what?*" Jiggs screamed. They were in the janitor's closet, and the room was filled with buckets, mops, and cleaning supplies.

"Not so loud," Charley hissed. "Someone might hear us."

"That is the absolute dumbest thing I ever heard," Jiggs continued in a softer voice, leaning against the paint-spattered sink.

"Well, it seemed like a good idea at the time," Charley protested weakly. Jiggs pulled a cord and a bare light bulb lit Charley's face from overhead.

"Now, let me see if I've got this straight," Jiggs began, pacing from the sink to the wall and back again. "Brett and all the rest of the dance class think you were a first-class jerk to Yvette, right?"

Charley nodded glumly.

"But you promised Yvette that you'd keep it all a secret until after the concert, the day after tomorrow."

"Right," Charley said. "And to top it all off,

Amanda is putting the moves on Brett." She slumped down onto a bucket in the corner. "She can have any boy she wants, and she picks mine!" Charley wailed.

"Well, you can't just sit there feeling sorry for yourself," Jiggs said firmly, her hands on her hips. "You've got to do something."

"Like what?"

"Like make a list of Amanda's assets and compare them with yours."

"Well, she's a senior, like Brett."

"And you're not."

"She's gorgeous, and she's a dynamite dresser."

"And you're not."

"Hey, you don't have to be so mean," Charley said, giving Jiggs a wounded look.

"Not the gorgeous part," Jiggs said quickly. "I meant the clothes part. Look at yourself, Charley. That outfit looks like you pulled it out of a laundry basket."

"I did," Charley admitted in a quiet tone.

"Well, tomorrow I want you to wash and iron your best outfit and wear it. Then curl your hair and put on a little makeup."

"But that takes so much time!" Charley protested. "Besides, if he doesn't like me the way I am—"

"Listen," Jiggs interrupted, grabbing a broom and brandishing it like a spear in the air. "This is *war*! You've got to fight fire with fire!"

"You're right!" Charley exclaimed, grabbing a mop. "I've got to beat her at her own game."

"That's right, you've got to pounce!"

"Pounce?" Charley asked, lowering her mop.

"If you don't let Brett know you care about him, somebody else will!"

"Like Amanda," Charley added, strangling her mop.

"That's the spirit!" Jiggs said with a laugh. Then she lowered her voice conspiratorially. "Now, the regional diving meet is this afternoon—"

"No kidding!" Charley put in grumpily. "It's all Amanda talks about."

"Well, you've *got* to be there."

Just then the bell on the wall right outside the closet rang loudly. Both girls shrieked and grabbed each other. Then they fell backward, knocking over the metal trash can. At the same moment, the closet door flew open.

"*What* is going on in here?" Mr. Pinsky, the school custodian, demanded.

"Charlotte was feeling faint," Jiggs said

quickly, pointing to Charley. "I thought a little water might help." She hastily turned on the faucet in the sink and tossed a handful of water at Charley.

"How do you feel now?" Jiggs asked with concern. "Better?"

"Oh, much better," Charley sputtered as the water dripped down her face. Then she mumbled through her teeth, "And I'll feel even better when we get out into the hall, and I can murder you."

"Good! Good!" Jiggs said, patting her on the shoulder. Charley reached for a paper towel and glared at her friend.

"Well, Mr. Pinsky," Jiggs said in a cheery voice, "we'd like to stay and chat, but we really have to get to class now."

She inched out the door and then turned and said pointedly, "Charley, if you don't feel any better by fifth period, you should go to the doctor."

The trash can had fallen over, so Charley daintily handed Mr. Pinsky the paper towel.

"Thanks for the use of your—uh—office, Mr. Pinsky."

"Just don't make a habit of it," he said gruffly, peering at her with twinkling eyes.

Charley ducked under his arm and pounded down the tiled hallway, completely forgetting that she was supposed to be terribly sick.

Chapter Eleven

By the time Charley finally made it over to the swimming pool that afternoon, the meet was well under way. The swimming and diving arenas were jammed with competitors and onlookers, all bustling from one event to the next. The same deafening noise she remembered from the first competition echoed all around her, but there was also something new—an intensity and a seriousness that the local meet hadn't had at all. It was unnerving, and Charley shuddered unconsciously from the tension.

Big banners were hung above the pool, proclaiming in large red letters: DALTON BEACH

WELCOMES THE WCF HIGH SCHOOL REGIONAL TOURNA-MENT. Teams from all over western Florida were clustered around the pool, and the only way to tell which was which was by the different-colored warm-up suits.

"Charley! *Char*-ley!" She jerked her head around at the sound of her name, trying to spot Jiggs in the confused jumble of people milling around her. Finally, up in the bleachers, she spotted her friend's familiar face.

"Over here!" Jiggs bellowed over the din. "I saved you a place!"

Charley nodded and threaded her way through the aisles. Finally she collapsed gratefully onto the empty seat Jiggs had held for her.

"Wow! It's a jungle out there!" she exclaimed.

"You're not kidding!" Jiggs agreed emphatically. "It looks as if half the state is here, not to mention most of the school."

Charley started to reply, but she suddenly saw Brett. He was toweling off by the Choctaw High bench and had obviously just finished a dive.

"Oh, no, Jiggs," Charley gasped in horror. "Don't tell me I've missed his dive!"

"Relax, Charley," her friend soothed. "If you'd been a few minutes later, I would have been worried, but as it is, you're just in time for the big finale."

"What do you mean? How's he doing? Is he ahead?" Charley's questions tumbled out so quickly that Jiggs held her hands up in mock horror.

"Whoa, one at a time!" she protested. Then she leaned toward her friend. "Here's the situation," she whispered. "It's come down to another duel between Brett and that guy from Pensacola—remember him? Scott Wren?"

Charley nodded her head nervously and motioned for Jiggs to go on.

"Well, it's getting scary—" She paused and looked awkwardly down at her feet. Charley's stomach did a nose dive, and she tugged at Jiggs's arm fiercely. "What is it? What's the matter?" she demanded.

Jiggs shot her a worried look. Then she blurted out, "Oh, Charley, you should have gotten here earlier! It was so exciting! Brett's first dives were brilliant. I mean, they were so brave and reckless and daring, he seemed to be dancing in the air. . . ." Her voice trailed off to a whisper. Charley couldn't bear it.

"What *happened*?" she practically screamed. The people who were sitting beside them gave her peculiar looks, but she didn't care.

"That's just it," Jiggs muttered in exasperation. "Nothing really wrong has happened. It's just that—well, it's like Scott Wren is a machine. Nothing fazes him. He is consistently perfect, and Brett seems to be—" She looked Charley square in the face. "Charley," Jiggs admitted quietly, "he's starting to blow it. His last dives haven't been as clean, as high, or as difficult as they should have been. It's like he's losing his confidence."

An uneasy silence hung between them for a moment. Then a burst of cheering went up from around the pool, and the noise sounded mocking and hollow in Charley's ears. She felt so frustrated.

"What can we do to help him?" she wondered out loud.

"It's not up to us," Jiggs answered, a note of determination entering her voice. "Wait a minute, it's not over yet. Brett can still win this thing. He just has to get back his control and dive the way he did at the beginning."

"Like when he was dancing," Charley murmured under her breath.

"What did you say?" Jiggs asked.

Charley shook her head and pointed down at the pool. They focused their attention on the diver mounting the board, Scott Wren. A teammate yelled out some last words of encouragement, and Scott waved back casually, as if diving were the easiest thing in the world. Charley glanced quickly over at Brett, who was sitting tensely with his towel wrapped around his neck, watching his rival's every move. His face was haunted and drawn in contrast to Scott Wren's easy smile.

Scott finally set his stance and began his approach down the board. The edge groaned and bent beneath his weight, then shot him skyward, and the crowd gasped in awe. It was an elegant display of diving technique. Each tuck and twist was precisely executed, and his entry into the water barely left a ripple across the surface. It was almost perfect.

"And yet . . ." Charley shook her head in irritation. She knew there was something wrong with Scott's dive, but she couldn't pin it down.

Meanwhile, Scott leaped out of the pool and swaggered back to his teammates, not even bothering to look back and wait for the judges to display his score. The crowd applauded as though he had won the competition, and a surge of anger shook Charley's body.

"How dare they act so confident! It's not over! Brett hasn't gone yet! He still has a chan—" Her words were drowned out by the roar that went up, as the judges displayed their scores. Scott Wren had received four 9.5s and a 10—one of the judges had given him a perfect score. A huge smile broke over his face, and he was surrounded by exultant teammates slapping him excitedly on the back. Even some of the spectators leaned over to congratulate him.

Jiggs looked over at Charley and shrugged helplessly, as if to say, "How can you beat that?" Charley looked back at Brett desperately. His coach was kneeling beside him, and Brett was listening intently, nodding now and then. There was a new firmness in his face, and it seemed as though there was more determination in the set of his jaw than before.

"You can do it, Brett!" Charley whispered over and over under her breath. Her hands were clasped so tightly that her knuckles were white with tension.

Brett reached the back of the diving platform and slowly ascended the steps. The crowd was still murmuring with excitement over Scott's dive, and the noise was not the respectful lull that had preceded everyone else's dives, but a disconcerting clamor. Charley remembered how a sound from the crowd had thrown Brett before, and the knot in her stomach grew tighter.

He stood patiently at the back of the board and waited for the noise to calm down. From where she was sitting, Charley felt as though she were looking straight into Brett's shining blue eyes. She held her breath as he began to run forward.

Suddenly, just before his take off, Brett stopped and wobbled precariously on the edge before regaining his balance. He walked quickly back to the railing.

"What happened?" Charley gasped.

"Something in the crowd must've distracted him," Jiggs said. "He's got to get his concentration back, and if he doesn't attempt the dive soon, he'll be disqualified!"

As though to emphasize Jiggs's point, an official walked up to the board and spoke to Brett, who just nodded. He stood still, grasping the steel railing with both hands, and stared intently out across the pool. Charley felt her heart tug in sympathy and frustration. It seemed as though he was looking right at her but couldn't see her.

Suddenly Brett's eyes flickered with recognition. *He knows it's me!* she thought in a rush.

Before she knew what she was doing, she smiled her bravest smile and, holding her hands high over her head, made the ballet sign for "Let's dance!"

His eyes didn't register the signal for a moment, then they snapped into focus, and a small smile crept across his face. He took a deep breath, and Charley could see the tension drain away from his neck and shoulders. He stepped forward and, without pausing, began his approach down the board.

As he ran down the narrow surface, it seemed as though time had slowed to a crawl. Charley watched each step in acute detail as Brett's thigh muscles contracted and then released with each step he took. Both feet came together perfectly for his release, and the board seemed to bend lower and lower, until Charley thought it would snap in two. But instead, it rebounded and rocketed him into the air.

Then, it looked as if Brett's upward motion would never stop. The height of his dive was incredible, and it seemed that he might hang in the sky forever. But a moment later, he spun and twisted effortlessly downward, whirling in an inspired concert of athletic grace and artistry.

And then it hit Charley: Brett wasn't just going through the moves mechanically; he made it look as if he were creating them for the first time. And that was the difference between Brett and Scott Wren. Scott was a skilled technician, but Brett was an artist. He was dancing in the air—and that made all the difference.

After he slipped into the water, the crowd seemed stunned for a few moments, as though they were unable to absorb what they had just seen. Charley looked at Jiggs, who was open-mouthed in awe.

"I don't believe I saw what I just saw," she stammered.

"Me, either," Charley whispered back. "But it *was* beautiful!"

Brett slipped his arms over one side of the pool and leaned against it with his eyes shut. On the other side, the judges were huddled together, whispering urgently. Then, with a nod of agreement, they sat back and flipped up their scorecards.

There, in a perfect row, were five 10s. All sorts of craziness broke loose. The Choctaw High team dove into the pool and mobbed Brett, who seemed dazed by it all. Then Scott Wren walked up to the side of the pool, held out his hand, and helped Brett onto the deck, congratulating him. Charley and Jiggs were jumping up and down, screaming with happiness.

Charley felt as if she would burst with pride. She knew that Brett had finally made it—now there was nothing to hold him back as a diver. And in a small way, she had helped him do it.

"I've got to congratulate him," she shouted to Jiggs, joining the crowd which was surging toward the new champion. Charley smiled inside at the memory of his recognizing her signal. She pressed forward eagerly and finally reached the aisle.

Brett had been lifted onto the shoulders of his teammates, who were carrying him triumphantly toward the awards platform. The crowd began to clap in unison and stomp their feet, and the whole arena resonated with the noise.

"Wasn't it exciting, Charley?" an all-too-familiar voice suddenly shouted in Charley's ear. Even before she turned to look, Charley knew it was Amanda. Before she could answer, however, Amanda rushed on breathlessly. "I mean, I thought he didn't have a chance before that last dive. It looked hopeless, didn't it?"

Charley nodded and tried to catch a glimpse of Brett through the crowd.

"But when I caught his eye and waved, he seemed to perk right up. And then he did that beautiful dive!"

"You *what?*" Charley spun around so quickly that Amanda stepped back with a startled look on her face.

"When I waved," Amanda repeated. "I knew he needed a boost," she explained. "So I showed him I was there. He was looking right at me, too!"

"But—but" Charley sputtered helplessly, "how could—I mean, it was me he—Where were you sitting?" she finished lamely.

"Skip Parker and I were right behind you and Jiggs in the bleachers," Amanda answered, a confused look clouding her face. Then her expression cleared, and she pushed by Charley into the surging crowd, squealing delightedly, "Oh, Brett! You were wonderful!"

Charley turned and caught a brief glimpse of Brett bouncing above the swirling heads and Amanda's upstretched arms. Then they both disappeared from view.

A terrible thought crossed Charley's mind. Maybe Brett hadn't seen her, after all. Maybe he'd made his perfect dive for Amanda instead. It seemed too horrible to contemplate, and yet the more she thought about it, the more it seemed possible. Boys always went for Amanda instead of her. Maybe she had just been kidding herself when she let herself think that she and Brett had something special together.

Suddenly Charley remembered that Jiggs was right beside her, and she turned to her pal for moral support. But one look at Jiggs's face confirmed her worst suspicions. She was looking back at Charley, concern and worry knitting her brow. Then her face brightened.

"Now listen to me," she said, obviously trying to see the situation in the most positive light. "This is just a minor setback."

"Minor!" Charley shouted over the noise.

"OK, so maybe it looks like a major setback," Jiggs admitted, linking her arm in Charley's as they walked out of the gym. "But you still have some cards in your hand."

"Like what?" Charley demanded impatiently.

"Like ballet class. And the concert," Jiggs explained. "There's no way Amanda can get involved in that!"

"You're right," Charley agreed, sighing with relief. "Tomorrow is our dress rehearsal, and we'll all be there for hours. Maybe I can find some time to talk to him then."

"And once he gets a look at you in your tutu, he'll fall admiringly at your feet!"

"Jiggs!" Charley said, rolling her eyes. "Everyone will be wearing a tutu!"

"But not like you wear a tutu!" Jiggs shot back, without missing a beat. "The minute he sees you, he'll forget all about Amanda."

Charley burst out laughing and hugged Jiggs with affection. "Oh, I wish I had your confidence!"

Jiggs grabbed her by the shoulders. "You do, Charley. You do," she said seriously.

Chapter Twelve

Charley stepped through the stage door and took a deep breath. To her, there was something wonderful about an empty theater; it was a place where anything could happen.

She walked across the wooden stage, listening to her footsteps reverberate in the huge room. Only a single rehearsal light lit the stage then, but in a few hours all the overhead lights would be on, and the pink-and-blue footlights would be directed on the dancers.

The big red curtain was drawn across the stage, waiting to be pulled back to reveal the magic that they would create, and a box of rosin had been placed on each side of the stage. The dancers would dust their toe shoes with the rosin to make sure they didn't slip.

For their concert, the setting was simple. The back wall was covered with a big blue cyclorama, a sheetlike curtain that looked like an endless sky. Charley dreamed that someday she would join a ballet company and, when they would perform ballets like *Giselle* and *Swan Lake*, the stage would be covered with gorgeous scenery instead of a blue curtain. But for now, she would have to be content with just the dancers and the music. She closed her eyes and could almost hear the violins.

Just then the stage door swung open again, and the air was filled with the high-pitched squeals of the younger ballet students. A few of their mothers were with them, instructing them to go downstairs to their dressing rooms.

Charley sighed, knowing that from then until ten o'clock that night, the theater would be organized chaos. Dress rehearsals were always like that. People would panic, not being able to find their costumes; the list showing the order in which they would perform would be posted, but no one would be able to read it; steps that had been rehearsed over and over in the studio would be forgotten in the excitement of doing them on a stage. Tempers would flare, too, but by the end of the evening, they would all be united in anticipation of opening night.

Charley found the dressing room that she and the other girls had been assigned and opened the door.

"Who took my eyeliner?" Marie cried, frantically searching the floor under the dressing table. "All right, you guys, cough it up!" she said, eyeing the other girls suspiciously.

"Did you check your makeup bag?" Julia asked from her chair at the end of the counter. Julia had neatly laid out a white-lace doily and carefully arranged her makeup on it. She was dressed in a pale-blue flowered kimono and was the only one in the whole room who seemed calm.

"Of course I checked my—" Marie stopped herself as her hand hit the eyeliner. "Oops," she said, smiling guiltily. "Sorry, everybody!"

"Lindsey, will you stop spraying that stuff?" Julia snapped. "It's giving me a headache."

"Sorry, but I have to put on a lot of hair spray," Lindsey snapped back. "You know how fine my hair is. If I don't spray it to death, it falls out on the first turn."

"But if you keep putting that junk on it, you won't have any hair left to spray by tomorrow night." Marie laughed.

"Have you ever considered varnish?" Julia muttered sarcastically. Lindsey pointedly ignored her and continued to cover her hair with spray.

"Charley, does my makeup look all right?" Marie asked, facing her.

"Well, the lines are a little thick, don't you think?" Charley said cautiously, trying to be diplomatic. She put her bag on her chair.

"A little!" Lindsey blurted out when she saw Marie. "It looks like she drew them on with a Magic Marker."

'And what are the red dots for?" Julia asked. "It looks like you have the measles."

"More like pinkeye!" Lindsey chortled.

Marie shot a pleading look at Charley. "You tell them!"

"Well," Charley explained, "red dots in the corners of your eyes are supposed to make your eyes look bigger. I don't know if it really works, but *all* the ballerinas do it."

All three girls suddenly reached for their red lip pencils and carefully placed a dot at the inside corner of each eye.

Charley slipped into the old terry cloth robe

she had brought to make up in, and laid out her things on the table in front of her mirror. Then she set a lavender glass bottle on the table.

"Ooh, what kind of perfume is that?" Lindsey asked.

"It's called Fleur de Lys," Charley said, squirting a little on her wrists.

"Just like our first dance number," Marie exclaimed.

"Uh-huh," Charley answered. "I saw it in the store and had to buy it. I thought it might bring me luck."

"Now, why didn't I think of that?" Marie moaned. "I'm going to need all the luck I can get."

Charley laughed and pinned her hair into a bun at the base of her neck. She put on her pale base makeup and then carefully outlined her eyes, extending the lines a little farther out for dramatic effect.

After everyone was finished, there was an awed silence, as all four girls looked at themselves in the mirror. The change was incredible. With their hair neatly pulled back and their makeup highlighting their features, they all looked like true ballerinas.

"Help!" Julia shrieked, breaking the silence.

"Someone has stolen my costume!" She frantically searched the pink tutus, looking for hers. "I knew something like this would happen."

For a moment they all gaped at her. Julia, for the first time, was losing her cool. She started tossing everyone else's costume onto the floor.

"Julia, calm down!" Charley shouted, springing to catch her tutu before it hit the ground. "I'm sure no one took your costume."

"Then where is it?" she demanded in a shaky voice.

Lindsey and Marie sprang into action and searched the racks. There were four costume changes during the concert, and everyone's outfits had been crammed onto two racks.

"Here it is!" Lindsey announced, holding up Julia's soft pink tutu proudly. "It accidently got put with some other costumes."

"Thanks," Julia muttered, reaching for her costume. "I guess I got a little nervous."

"A little!" Marie gloated, picking her tutu up off the floor. "Boy, if this is how you are at a dress rehearsal, what are you going to be like at the real performance!"

Julia started to flare up again, but the sound of Mrs. Klein's voice interrupted her.

"Ten minutes until you have to be in your places!" she called pleasantly.

"*Ten minutes!*" they all chorused back. The dressing room suddenly became a madhouse as they battled one another for their costumes and tried to pull on their tights and shoes in the cramped space.

Charley was dressed first and managed to slip out of the room ahead of the others. In the hall she paused to look at herself in the full-length mirror.

The pink satin bodice that was cut to a point at the waist showed off her pretty shoulders. The skirt flowed out in net and chiffon to just below the knee. It was the classic "ballerina length." She made a light leap and watched the skirt respond like a soft pink cloud around her legs.

Yvette peeked out of her dressing room and rushed over to hug Charley.

"You look beautiful!" Yvette gushed.

"So do you!" Charley said, stepping back to look at her new friend. "You make a perfect Juliet."

The velvet bodice of Yvette's costume fit her frail frame beautifully, and white chiffon billowed delicately from the empire waist. A tiny silver braid crowned her hair.

"Come on," Charley whispered. "Let's go over to the stage before the others get there."

They tiptoed quickly up the stairs and through the wings.

"Tomorrow night, all those seats will be filled," Charley whispered to Yvette as they peeked out from behind the curtain at the auditorium.

"Oh, Charley, I don't know if I'll be able to go through with this," Yvette cried, her face looking increasingly panicked.

"Of course you will. The pas de deux is beautiful, and having an audience will just make it complete," Charley reminded her.

"Just remember to pick one person and dance for him or her," Brett said, stepping onto the stage from the wings.

Charley felt her knees go weak, and she swallowed hard. He looked just like a prince—his white tights showing off his muscular thighs, and the blue velvet doublet making his eyes sparkle.

"Brett's right," she said, squeezing Yvette's hand extra hard. She was unable to take her eyes off him.

Then she suddenly gasped and stepped back, remembering their secret. "You're on your own," she mumbled, but Brett was grinning from ear to ear.

"You two look absolutely fantastic," he said. Charley started to back away in confusion, but Yvette stopped her.

"It's OK, Charley. Brett knows," Yvette whispered with a smile. "I had to tell him. I couldn't bear having everyone think so badly of you. Besides, he had a right to know why I was getting so much better."

Charley was so relieved to have everything out in the open that she didn't know whether to laugh or cry. Finally she went with the urge to laugh and threw her head back, giggling for all she was worth. Soon Yvette began to laugh, too, and then Brett joined in. The three of them stood in a circle giggling and patting one another on the back. Their laughter was interspersed with cries of "I thought that you thought . . ." and "You should have seen your face!"

"Well, what have we here?" Julia called from the edge of the stage. The rest of the dancers had gathered behind her and were all watching the scene wide-eyed. "It seems that Miss Maclaine has finally accepted the fact that she is just a member of the corps!"

"That's right," a calm voice echoed behind

her. "And you would do well to take a lesson from her, Miss Julia Taylor!"

Everyone froze as Miss Carabelli stepped onto the stage. She was elegantly dressed in a flowing black gown and black high heels. Striding to the center of the curtain, she eyed them all sternly.

"Girls, your attention, please," she commanded. "Before we begin the rehearsal, I have a little announcement to make."

The dancers shifted and squirmed uncomfortably, wondering what she was going to say.

"The life of a ballerina is a difficult one. It is filled with much hard work, long hours of practice, and many aching muscles. It also means always striving for perfection, and it can be very lonely." Miss Carabelli got a faraway look in her eyes, and Charley and the other girls kept a respectful silence, suddenly realizing what her life must have been like.

"For this reason, it is important to remember your fellow artists—to be kind and help them whenever you can. In that is the true spirit of a dancer. Charlotte," she continued, turning to face Charley, "I have watched you closely over these past weeks, and . . ."

She paused, and Charley's stomach fell. *Uh*

oh, here it comes. She's going to lecture me.

"I am so very proud of you." Miss Carabelli's face broke into a broad smile. "Your unselfishness in helping Yvette proves that you have grown, not only as a dancer, but as a person."

The other girls gasped and stared at Charley's bewildered face.

"There are no secrets in my studio," Miss Carabelli added, laughing lightly. "You may not believe it, but I have seen you both working so diligently each morning."

Charley and Yvette shot each other stunned looks. They had thought they were alone.

"For this reason, I have decided to make a change in the recital."

All of the girls started murmuring in worried tones.

"Don't worry, nothing will be removed. However, I will be making one small addition. Charley, the solo you have been working on from *Sleeping Beauty* will be added to the program."

"What?" Charley shouted. "But Miss Carabelli, I—"

"Do you feel confident that you know it well enough?" Miss Carabelli interrupted in a concerned tone.

"Of course I do," Charley squealed. "I've been practicing it every day for months."

"I thought so." Miss Carabelli smiled. "But?"

"But it's just that—" Charley stammered. Then she blurted out, "I—I don't have a costume."

"Ah! I have thought of that," Miss Carabelli said, walking toward the wings. As soon as she had disappeared, the other girls swarmed all over Charley.

"Charley, this is wonderful!" Yvette gushed, hugging her proudly. "You deserve it!"

"Boy, you two sure put one over on us!" Marie said, punching Charley's arm. Then she whispered, "Where can I get some of that lucky perfume?"

"Congratulations, Charley," Julia said reluctantly. She had an I-wish-I-had-helped-Yvette look on her face.

Charley was still speechless. As Lindsey and some other girls hugged her, she could see Brett watching her and smiling. He caught her eye and winked, which sent another thrill of happiness through her. She wanted to say something to him, but she was too giddy to think straight, and everything seemed to be whirling around her.

Miss Carabelli walked back onto the stage

carrying a worn but beautiful wardrobe box. A hushed silence came over the group as every single eye became glued to the box. Miss Carabelli lifted the lid, removed some tissue, and carefully revealed the prize that was inside.

"Oh, it's beautiful!" the girls exclaimed at once. Charley's mouth dropped open as she saw the incredible costume.

It was a fluffy white tutu, more exquisite than anything she had ever seen. The bodice was made of pale white velvet, covered in tiny pearls and opals that glowed softly, even in the dim light of the single bulb above them. Even tinier pearls had been delicately sewn in between the layers of netting. But the most beautiful part of all was the sparkling green emerald at the center of the bodice.

"Oh, Miss Carabelli," Charley whispered, "I couldn't wear this. It's too beautiful!"

"I wore this at my final performance as a prima ballerina," Miss Carabelli murmured fondly, cradling the tutu in her arms. "It seems a shame to let it sit in a box for all these years." She carefully handed it to Charley, her eyes glistening. "I would be most proud if you would wear it."

Charley took the magnificent costume from

her teacher's hands and held it in her arms.
The bubble that had been building up inside
her for so long burst wide open. Charley began to cry big, wet tears of joy.

Chapter Thirteen

As Charley drove through the deserted streets of Dalton Beach, she pinched herself to make sure she wasn't dreaming. So much had happened so fast that she hadn't really absorbed it all. Charley shook her head in amazement at how quickly everything had turned around for her. She had gotten a solo—and a beautiful costume to dance it in. It was as if she had wandered into a fairy tale. In spite of all the frustration and disappointment of the past few weeks, everything had turned out all right.

Only one thing would have made it all perfect—Brett.

She whispered his name softly to the full moon glowing above her. Just saying his name made her spine tingle. Sadly, she remembered that she hadn't gotten a chance to talk to him after Miss Carabelli's surprise announcement. The dress rehearsal had begun almost immediately, and then Miss Carabelli had insisted that Charley stay after all the others had gone home to run through her solo again.

She shook her head impatiently.

You've got to stop mooning over him like some love-struck idiot, she warned herself. *It just didn't work out, that's all. These things happen. You can't have everything you want, you know.*

She turned the car around the corner onto her street and sighed. All the talking in the world couldn't change the fact that she'd have traded the solo in a minute for a chance to be with Brett.

Charley pulled into her driveway, parked the car, and headed toward the back door. When she stepped into the kitchen, Amanda was there waiting for her.

"I've had about as much as I can stand from you!" her sister said, fuming. "I won't put up with it anymore!"

"What are you complaining about now?" Charley mumbled distractedly.

"Brett just called—"

"Brett?" Charley interrupted.

"Yes, Brett!" Amanda shot back. "I have practically killed myself trying to get his attention, and all he talks about is *you!*"

"What!" Charley exclaimed, flabbergasted. "What does he say?"

" 'Charley this,' and 'Charley that!' " Amanda mimicked and walked airily upstairs toward their bedroom.

"Amanda, please!" Charley squealed, following her sister. "Tell me what he said."

She heard Amanda rummaging around in her closet, muttering to herself. Finally Amanda turned back toward Charley.

"I'm turning in my equipment," she announced dramatically. She dropped a pair of jogging shorts, matching headband, and running shoes on the floor in front of Charley with a clatter.

"You can have it! If I never run another block, it'll be fine with me."

"Amanda," Charley asked, staring at her sister, "did he want to talk to me?"

Amanda stared at Charley as though she were an alien from Mars.

"Of course he did," she said emphatically. "Haven't you heard a word I just said?" Amanda tossed her hands up in disbelief. "He wanted to talk to you. Not me, *you!*"

"*Amanda!*" Charley yelled. "What did he want?"

"Didn't I tell you?" Amanda exclaimed, dropping her arms to her sides.

"No, you didn't," Charley said, with as much patience as she could muster, trying to stifle the urge to scream.

"I guess I'm just so rattled by the guy that I can't think straight," Amanda muttered. "I still can't get over it. I have tried every trick in the book, and—"

"*Amanda!*" Charley screamed, shaking her sister by the shoulders. "*Tell me what he said!*"

"Well, you don't have to get pushy about it," Amanda said and sniffed primly. "He just said that if you got home before eleven o'clock, he'd like to talk to you at the usual place. He said something about needing your help."

"It's five minutes to eleven!" Charley cried, looking at her watch. "Why didn't you tell me sooner? He's going to leave."

"Not Brett." Amanda smiled knowingly. "That guy is stuck on you. I should know, because that's all I've heard for the last two weeks. He'll probably wait all night. Now, why can't I get a guy to do that for me?"

"Amanda, you have practically every boy in school wrapped around your little finger!" Charley yelled over her shoulder as she flew toward the back door.

"That's true," Amanda mused, smiling with satisfaction.

"Amanda?" Charley asked, pausing at the door. "Wish me luck, OK?"

Amanda's face suddenly softened. Then she charged over to Charley and hugged her.

"You don't need luck, Charley," she whispered. "You're already a winner!"

"Thanks, Mandy," Charley said, starting to hug her back.

Amanda broke away and, with an embarrassed laugh, cracked, "You'd better hurry, or someone else may get to Brett first!"

Then, with a good-natured shove, she sent Charley flying through the door and out into the moonlit night.

Charley's heart pounded in her throat as she dashed up over the last dune. She was so afraid she'd be too late, that Amanda was just teasing her, or that it was all too good to be true.

But he was there! Brett's dark figure stood silhouetted against the phosphorescent glow of the surf tumbling up before them. The moon had transformed the sand and sky into a silvery tapestry of flickering light.

"Brett!" Charley's voice rang out in the night.

"Hi," Brett replied as he trotted toward her. "I was hoping you'd come."

"I came as fast as I could after I got your message." Charley was winded from running, and she bent over to catch her breath.

Brett stood there a moment, smiling at her. Then he ran his hand through his hair and laughed.

"Gee, now that I've got you here, I'm not sure what to say."

"Amanda said you needed my help?" Charley responded, still clutching her side.

"Huh?" Brett looked confused for a moment. "Oh, yeah, that!"

"Well?" Charley prodded, tilting her head slightly.

"Well, it's about—" He dug his heel in the sand. "It's about the pas de deux! I'm a little confused about a few of the moves."

Charley dropped her arms to her sides and stared at him. *This is why he wanted to see me so badly? To help him with the dance? Miss Carabelli could have helped him. Anyone could've helped him.*

"Well," Charley shrugged, "I don't know. I got a chance to watch from the wings tonight, and it looked pretty good to me."

"I don't know." Brett shook his head. "Something's missing."

"What?" Charley asked, trying to remember if they'd made any mistakes.

"I'm not sure," Brett explained. "Maybe if you could go over it with me, I'd figure it out." He looked at her with his gorgeous blue eyes, and Charley melted.

"Sure," she smiled. "From where?"

"Let's start with the arabesque." He held out his hand, and Charley grasped it and rose up on half point with one leg extended high behind her.

"From here?" she asked, lifting her chin to look at him.

"That's right." Brett stepped behind her, placing his hands lightly on her waist. "This is the point where Romeo first realizes how much he cares for Juliet," he said.

Brett spoke softly, almost whispering into her ear, and Charley could feel a tingling sensation run down her back.

"He can't take his eyes off her," Brett continued.

"Yes?" Charley whispered expectantly.

"They dance, moving in and out of each other's arms." Brett twirled her away from him, and Charley skipped lightly back. She circled around him, following the steps that Miss Carabelli had taught them.

"But Romeo hesitates," Brett said, stepping back and covering his heart with his hand. "He's unsure of how she feels about him."

"But Juliet fell for him the moment she saw him," Charley blurted out.

"She did?" Brett perked up, taking a step toward her.

"Yes," Charley whispered, gazing into his eyes.

She quickly changed her tone and added, "But Juliet isn't sure how Romeo feels."

"He wants to tell her but doesn't know how," Brett said.

"Maybe he should just—just say it!" Charley sputtered.

"Maybe he's shy," Brett responded quietly. "And can't find the right words."

They both realized they'd stopped dancing and were staring at each other. The surf ebbed and flowed around their ankles.

"So," Brett said gruffly, clearing his throat, "he tells her in the only way he knows how."

Brett raised his hands above his head and twirled them in the motion for "Let's dance." It was the same signal she'd given him at the diving meet!

"Oh, Brett," Charley cried, her eyes glistening. "That's the most wonderful thing anyone's ever said to me!"

Brett laughed, a big, warm laugh that filled the darkness. He threw his arms open wide.

Charley raced toward him, and he caught her around the waist, lifting her high over his head. They froze there for one sparkling moment, and then he slowly lowered her down into his strong arms.

They looked into each other's eyes, and then their lips met, softly, without hesitation. Brett drew her closer to him.

As he leaned down to kiss her again, Miss Carabelli's words echoed in her mind: *There is nothing more exquisite than two people dancing as one: one body, one heart, one soul.*

ANNOUNCING THE SPECTACULAR

ALL THAT GLITTERS

SWEEPSTAKES

It's part of the hot new series **ALL THAT GLITTERS**. In each book you'll meet the cast of the sensational soap opera **ALL THAT GLITTERS** and share the joys and heartaches as they balance their acting careers with the ups and downs of teenage life.

THREE CHANCES TO WIN!

Not just Book #1, but **Books #2 & 3 as well** offer you a chance at fabulous prizes! In the back of each book will be a question about that story—and if you are among the first five hundred to submit a correct entry you will win a fantastic ALL THAT GLITTERS "EARLY BIRD PRIZE". 1500 PRIZES—500 EARLY BIRD PRIZES AWARDED FOR EACH BOOK!

BUT THE BEST IS YET TO COME!

Every correct entry from the three books will be entered in our Grand Prize Sweepstakes—and the winner will win A TRIP FOR TWO TO NEW YORK CITY (3 DAYS/2 NIGHTS) INCLUDING HOTEL ... TRANSPORTATION AND DINNERS.

No purchase necessary. Sweepstakes ends December 31st, 1987. Entry blanks and official rules will be found in the back of MAGIC TIME #1, TAKE TWO #2, and FLASHBACK #3 or see special displays wherever books are sold for complete details, including alternative means of entry.

Don't miss your chance! Book #1, Magic Time, will be on sale in September—and watch closely for Book #2 (on sale October) and Book #3 (on sale November)

ALL THAT GLITTERS

It's Hot!